"*The Cracks We Bear* is a beautiful work of memory and image craftsmanship. What does anyone know about being a mother? the book seems to scream at us. And there is no answer, only a woman's search in the face of the abyss of her motherhood. Behind this book lies a poetic and intimate truth: there are no complete stories, only pieces, fragments, and often the work of writing is not to reveal what is missing but to preserve it within the word as a secret."
NATALIA GARCÍA FREIRE, author of *A Carnival of Atrocities*

"Reflective, sensitive, and often moving, Catalina Infante's first novel revolves around a mother-daughter relationship, its silences, distances, and cracks."
La Tercera

"A poignant story, full of touching moments that approach motherhood from a more human perspective. It addresses the fears, exhaustion, and disappointment of first-time mothers who feel suffocated by overwhelming social mandates. Catalina Infante constructs a vision of motherhood that is terrifying, and describes a facet of motherhood that is not portrayed in magazines, TV shows, or movies."
Infobae

"A literary composition somewhere between a confessional diary and a costumbrista's work that portrays society with some sarcasm, but also with the necessary dose of tenderness and hope. The author outlines, with a beautifully feminine intimacy, the shaken Chile of the last thirty years. The novel gives voice to an uprooted Chilean daughter of political

exiles, in search of her own intimate identity, in a country that was foreign to her from the very moment of her birth."
Cine y Literatura

"A very personal, intimate book that explores longings, doubts, tiredness, and social pressures connected to motherhood, and the need to return to normality, to recover oneself, one's own body."
Bio Bio Chile

"Catalina Infante writes with empathy about loneliness, grief, fears, exile, motherhood, and the relationship of mothers with feminism."
Culturizarte

"When her daughter Antonia is born, Laura thinks of Esther, her mother. A mother who was not especially loving, who thought the best inheritance was a good education. A mother with whom Laura had many differences, and who died from cancer when she was eighteen. Laura finds photos and postcards that Esther never sent; she relives vague and elusive moments in her memory, and discovers that she did not know the woman who lived in her mother."
La Tercera

"*The Cracks We Bear* is a 'real,' concrete, human story full of small details … a story about being a daughter, and a mother, in a society that idealizes motherhood."
Futuro

The Cracks We Bear

CATALINA INFANTE

The Cracks We Bear

Translated from the Spanish
by Michelle Mirabella

WORLD EDITIONS
New York

Published in the USA in 2025 by World Editions NY LLC, New York

World Editions
New York

Original title *La grieta*

Printed by Lightning Source, USA

Library of Congress Cataloging in Publication Data is available

ISBN 978-1-64286-159-4

Company: worldeditions.org
Facebook: @WorldEditionsInternationalPublishing
Instagram: @WorldEdBooks
TikTok: @worldeditions_tok
Twitter: @WorldEdBooks
YouTube: World Editions

My senses are yours,
and with this as the gift of your flesh,
I make my way through the world.

GABRIELA MISTRAL
TR. MARIA GIACHETTI

1

The day Antonia was born, just hours before heading to the hospital, I dug desperately through every box in the house in search of my mother's little Santa Teresa medal. Esther was an atheist, but for some reason believed that Santa Teresa was her guardian. The medal was something she'd always put on when she was afraid to face things, and that day I couldn't find it. I'd most likely lost it when Felipe and I moved into this house, the same house I'd lived in with her when I was a little girl. Later at the hospital, in the moments of respite from my animalistic screams, I thought of that medal with rage, and I thought of my mother with rage, asking myself why she wasn't there giving birth with me.

As for her things, I don't have many; I've lost almost all of them. It's not often I lose things, but when it comes to hers, I do. They stray from me, abandon me, as if everything of hers were doomed to disappear. When people ask me about the medal, I say: my mother gave it to me. But that's not true; she wasn't one to give me her things. I just stole it out of her closet a few months after she died. Left there were her pockets stuffed with bits of paper, her perfumed clothing, her worn-out shoes, and the box full of pictures and postcards she'd written while in exile. From time to time, I'd open that closet and rummage through it all, tossing the boxes and purses every which way in search of her, just in case she was in there, hidden among the receipts or in her scrawl on a half-written check. During one of those intrusions on her memory, I picked up the medal and put it on. I made a promise to myself that I don't recall in detail, but it had to do with my resolve not to let the pain define me—to have it disappear. And somehow it did. Over the years, the pain left me, just like her things.

When Felipe sees me holding Antonia as I pace around this house, around her room which is now our room, he asks me, do you miss her? I never know what to say. You don't just miss a mother who dies; it's another emotion, difficult to name. Perhaps there's a word for it in another language, a grouping of letters whose sound can hold such emptiness. We just learn to live like this, half broken, as if an organ has been removed from our bodies, leaving a hole in its place. You feel stalled out, but the body learns to function, and you suddenly find that life feels normal.

When I came home from the hospital, without Santa Teresa but with Antonia, that hole grew even darker. What do I know about being a mother? Absolutely nothing. I asked myself that question and so many others as Antonia cried and my delivery wound ached deeply with pain and motherhood hit me blindside. I ask the question of myself, if I miss her, and I still don't know what to say. I place a picture of her on my nightstand to anchor her in my mind, fearing that one day I'll wake up and the memory of her will have faded. I look at the picture when I want to remember what it was like to have a mother, for there to be someone in this world who holds you so completely. But when I look at her, I'm reminded that such unconditional support isn't real, it never truly existed. That's what we believe when we're little girls, that it must be absolute. But we mothers know that's not true, and we dwell silently in that distance.

I think of how terrifying motherhood is; it was never like they told us it would be. The world tells itself one story and only we mothers know the other.

2

I wanted a natural birth—squatting, in the dark, with the image of myself pulling my bloody daughter out and placing her on my chest. That's how Esther had me, in a hospital in Paris, but not by choice; the use of anesthesia was not common practice among the French. They'd have the baby and that was that, she'd say. For me, it was different. After two days of contractions, I received Antonia while splayed out on a metal table, trembling with fear, surrounded by five people working to put my flesh back in place.

I did everything I was supposed to do. I read all the books on the topic: the ones saying the pain is cultural, the testimonies from women who orgasmed on the last push, books about deliveries guided by doulas who, like Greek goddesses, support you in your transition to motherhood. I meditated, recited mantras, stretched my pelvis daily. Felipe and I planned out the birth in detail, to sort out any obstacles that could cause us stress or sway me from my path. I wanted to be able to move and scream; I wanted a limited number of people and limited words, so that my oxytocin would fill everything with strength—and all those other things we were promised in classes. But I didn't dilate. Who can dilate when everyone is waiting for them to dilate?

The doctor convinced me to accept the synthetic hormones and my contractions went from manageable to excruciatingly painful. Felipe told me that on my last scream the look on my face was primal, and I feared my own intensity. The doctor told us that Antonia had dislodged; her head was hitting against my pelvis, and she would never come out of there. And that's how my body felt, shut tight like a stubborn clam. At midnight, after two days of no sleep, the anesthesiologist switched on the lights in the room, as if to say show's over, and injected me with a gigantic needle. They took Felipe to don the green-colored scrubs and laid me out on a table that resembled two outstretched arms; I threw mine open. Please, I yelled, don't tie me down! No one had any intention of doing so. But just having the restraints there, close to my arms, made a menace of that place. Why am I trembling? I asked the midwife. It's the anesthesia, she replied. But it was fear. The nurses prattled on about something useless, a doctor answered texts on his phone, and I seethed with rage thinking of all those stories they told at the workshops about women subjected to unnecessary C-sections.

When they pulled Antonia from my open body, I looked up at her swollen, purpled face and felt tiny in her presence. When they laid her on my chest, she stared right at me with the magnanimity of an empress, as if piercing every dimension of my minuscule existence. Afterwards, Felipe and I would talk about that first impression and call it Medusa's gaze: Antonia, with serpents in her hair, and the two of us, petrified. She squirmed like an animal and latched on to my breast, master of my body, while the doctor shook out my skin as if shaking dust from a blanket. As I clutched her to me, we were rolled through the hospital, pushed through its corridors and into its elevators, until we arrived at a transition room where there was another mother in shock. I was still trembling. I was a girl back there, I thought, a little girl giving birth. My sacrum didn't budge, and I never felt that ring of fire at my vaginal opening, like the books said I would; I was weak, passive, stripped of all power. But who am I to judge myself—myself or any mother? Our decisions don't tend to be ours to make; what we control is practically nil.

3

I take a seat on the only shaded bench in the plaza, with Antonia squeezed against me in a poorly tied baby wrap. This time of day is quiet in the park. Sometimes other zombie mothers like me shuffle through with their newborns. Toward the far side of the plaza, a group of older women keep an eye on some young children whose mothers, I imagine, have already gone back to work. The owner of Pimienta, a German Shepherd mutt that comes over every morning to sniff at me, is a new mother as well. While we were pregnant, we'd talk in this same plaza seeking the comfort of someone with shared experience. Now, months later, she looks haggard, pinched, with bags under her bulging eyes. Coursing through her is that adrenaline of the first few months, an emergency trance that we women enter into as if the world were going up in flames around us. She tells me that she's lost twenty-five pounds in four weeks because she doesn't have time to eat. She doesn't sleep either; I know because her appearance mirrors mine. She has these meager ten minutes to walk the dog before her husband leaves for work and is gone until nightfall. Ten minutes she uses to vent to me: the baby screams all day and cries while nursing, my milk is not enough. I'd like to help her with all that, but I'm no better off. Since Antonia was born, I haven't slept more than three hours in a row. It's hard for me to think. I say goodbye to Pimienta and her owner, and at the departing sounds of that desperate voice, Antonia wakes up screaming. Flustered, I run home to guess at how to soothe her cries.

Felipe and I decided to move into my mother's house, the same one she and I had lived in together, but now with different furniture, different colors on the walls, a different life. I was a bit resistant to the idea of returning, but Felipe convinced me that it had more space for us, and a patio, which is impossible to afford in Santiago today. I hadn't stepped foot in this house for more than a decade. After Esther died, I continued living here for a time; I rented out my room to an exchange student and I used Esther's. I left her things in the closet for a while: her shoes, a few purses, the clothing she bought before she died and never had a chance to wear. I locked the closet until I could figure out what to do with it all. I was never able to wear any of her things because she was bigger, taller than me. Even so, from time to time, I'd try something on in hopes that it would suddenly fit; the mirror reflected back a small, hidden body in an endless costume. When I finished university, I bagged up her clothing and went to the church of Santa Teresa to donate it. The woman at the church told me they didn't need clothing, that they had too much clothing as it was, and shut the door in my face. I took the five garbage bags out of the taxi anyway and left them in the front garden, where bored churchgoers bided their time until Mass was over, and quickly ran out of there without looking back. Then I rented out the house, and in all this time I hadn't had anything to do with it, until I got pregnant with Antonia, and we decided to return.

In the mornings, Felipe's mother comes over to help me and then I spend the afternoons at home arranging things to make the house feel different, but more than anything I'm washing dishes, changing diapers, cleaning up the chaos, and looking at my phone. Felipe comes home early from work to look after Antonia, and I take the opportunity to go on a walk around the block, to the supermarket, anywhere, to regain something of myself that I'm not so sure I want back. Some afternoons, as Antonia sleeps, I look through the pictures and postcards in Esther's box, unsure of what it is that I'm hoping to find.

4

My mother's family didn't have much. That's what she'd always told me, ever since I was a little girl. She was born in a village in Valle del Choapa, lived there until she was eighteen, and then came to Santiago to work as a secretary. Here, she met my father, a pije revolucionario, as she called him—a revolutionary snob studying to be a teacher. She went into exile for that pije, first to Cuba for four years and then to France, where she managed to get into university and have a better time of it. She was never happy in Europe; at least not the way she was in Cuba. I didn't know that from her but from reading the postcards in her box, which are seemingly addressed to no one but herself. *I feel like I'm in a white jail*, she writes in one of them. Even so, she'd tell me stories of it as a dreamlike place. We lived near a castle in Chantilly, outside of Paris, beside a forest where the deer would walk through the snow in winter. *You were born into privilege, Laura, you have no idea what it is to suffer.*

My father lost his mind in France. He was always a bit unstable, but there, she said, he hit rock bottom. One time, she told me, he spent weeks digging a hole in the back patio of our house while refusing to speak to anyone or answer any questions. When my mother was at her wit's end and begged him to stop, he admitted he was planning to hide underground for a few months because they were looking for him, that he'd breathe through a tube, he'd trained for this. That's when my mother realized that things were a bit more than off.

Of their love story I don't know much, just the basics, because he's scatterbrained and she didn't like to remember. In the nineties they separated for good, with some dramatic incidents I don't remember, but there they are, etched in the family body. My mother decided to return to Chile with me and secured a job as a professor at a French private school for the upper class. I went to school there on scholarship alongside other children who'd returned to Chile and a bunch of rich kids who wanted to be French. We'd raise the flag singing "La Marseillaise" and were forbidden from stepping foot on the great lawn behind the flagpole because Charles de Gaulle had been there, which meant it was sacred.

At first my father would write and call often, then he gradually faded from our lives until he was nothing more than a stranger. Some of his postcards are in the box too; he'd send me pictures or absurd drawings where he'd write phrases in French to make me laugh, or perhaps test my language skills. *On dirait une grosse légume*, on the back of a drawing of a voluptuous woman. *Comme cul et chemise!* on the back of two dogs drinking a coffee. To this day Michel sells antiques. He drives a pickup truck to auctions all over France and lives with a friend—that friend, Esther would say—in the same house where I was born. Now we only see each other when he comes to Chile, and he insists on giving me the child support money he owes from all those years. The historical debt he calls it, laughing, during a forced conversation in which I tell him vaguely of my life and he tells me little of his own. When our clipped dialogue begins to make him uncomfortable, he says things like *parle-moi en français* and I respond with I hate French and he says then why did I pay for your schooling, and I tell him you paid for nothing. Then he throws himself back with a laugh, arms spread wide, as if he's falling out of his chair.

5

Felipe's sleeping on the armchair in the living room to give us a bit of space, which I do appreciate, but it makes me indignant. I envy his freedom to walk away without consequence. At night, when she cries, I turn away and feign sleep to see if she'll settle back down, despite knowing full well that it never works. The only place she'll sleep is on me, exclusively on my right side, between my arm and my breast. When she finally does fall asleep, then I'm the one who can't. Being unable to move makes me anxious, but so does the thought of moving and waking her up again. At a certain point we both succumb to sleep for a few hours—never more than three. I wake up with half my body numb, and she smiles without yet knowing what it means to smile. Felipe comes to relieve me. I pass out until he goes to work and his mother arrives, ever impertinent but willing, full of an affection for the two of us that never ends. Or that lasts at least until midday when she goes off to do her own thing. In the afternoons, Antonia and I cook together with her snug in the baby wrap, play with the same toys and their same few songs, and try not to turn on the TV because they say it's bad for babies' brains, even though we always end up watching BabyTV to get some rest—Felipe doesn't know. Then it's a struggle in the tub because she can't stand the water, and I feel like I hate her. When Felipe gets home from work we hardly acknowledge each other; I just hand off Antonia so I can go take a shower. When I was pregnant, I'd take long baths and relish the soap's fragrance—it would give me a dizzying thrill. Now when I shower I'm jumpy, hearing phantom cries, anxious to rinse out the shampoo and hurry back to holding her, because I miss her. On good afternoons, Felipe manages to get Antonia to sleep in her room; she takes a long, four-hour nap, giving us time to be together, like before. We try to watch a show, talk, kiss, nothing works. We just collapse exhausted, clinging to each other, petrified. Then Antonia cries. Felipe brings her over to me in our bed and heads to the armchair to sleep. I get anxious watching him walk away; I'd like for us to stay here wrapped in each other's arms, sleeping deeply, still as stones.

6

My friend Blanca was expecting me for lunch, and I didn't show up. Ten missed calls and a message that says: *you're unbelievable.* Whenever I go to Blanca's—something I haven't had the energy to do since Antonia was born—her parents come for lunch. It's our ritual, as if we were family. They've been asking nonstop to come ever since I went in to the hospital, but I haven't wanted anyone over. It's overwhelming to see people anxious to hold her, and to field all their questions—I'm too tired to answer. I'm also tired of explaining my overwhelm, so I just say yes to everything and then cancel, using whatever excuse. But excuses don't work with Blanca, she knows me too well, since we were eleven years old.

Her father was head of a major underwear line in Los Angeles until they transferred him to Chile. As soon as Blanca arrived at my school—her mother has French heritage—they sat us together in classes, and we wouldn't stop talking. This was only a problem for me because her grades were outstanding, and I was just scraping by. They lived in a nineties yuppie neighborhood in a building with a hotel-style lobby and a home that looked like a model apartment. They'd eat pancakes for breakfast, make popcorn on weekends, and watch movies together. To me, they were perfect. They'd tell me stories about their vacations in Florida, and I made their memories into my own. Blanca would invite me to her house on Fridays and her parents would end up asking me to stay until Sunday. I imagine because I was her only friend, and they were happy she was adjusting so quickly to Chile. I'd only bring enough clothing for one day—I didn't want the embarrassment of showing up with a big bag if they ever grew tired of me. But they never did. Her father would bring home a set of underwear from the office as a gift in case I didn't have enough with me, as if making it clear I was part of the clan. The set, always white, came in what looked like a small, oval cookie tin, and included a training bra. Esther never bought me bras. You've got nothing there, she'd say, so using them at Blanca's felt like a victory. I liked being part of their family dynamic in that apartment where the food never went bad, and it always smelled of fake fruit. Her mother let us watch TV, but not too much, made us eat at the table, never in bed, and would get upset if we used bad words. She was strict, and I liked that. She'd get us up early on Sundays for Mass, even me, although she knew Esther and I were atheists. Then we'd wait for Blanca's father, who was off playing golf, and we'd have chicken and french fries, ketchup and Coca-Cola, something Esther would have never allowed. At the end of the day, her father would offer to drop me off, but early, because we had school the next day and there's homework to do, he'd say. We'd all get into the car together, and my stomach would sink with that feeling you get when something bad is about to happen. But it was just guilt for having masqueraded in a life not my own. My mother never liked Blanca's family; perhaps they made her feel like her love was not enough. And perhaps I thought that too, but I never could've said that to her. We didn't have that kind of relationship, the kind where mother and daughter talk about love. The illusion of that borrowed life would always fade as Blanca's father made the turn onto Avenida Grecia. With that silent movement of the steering wheel I'd recall Esther's word of warning: the capitalist promise, the one ensuring that where things looked beautiful they were good and where things looked ugly they were inadequate, was a lie, a mirage. When I'd get out of the car, Esther wouldn't be outside waiting for me—as a punishment, I think. I'd use my own key to get into the house and shut myself in the bathroom to take off the bra. When I'd come out, I'd find her lying there watching the news, the cats on top of her, in a darkness that remained even when the lights were on. Although the bulbs were the same as the ones in Blanca's house, in mine they failed to illuminate the space; all they did was cast dark shadows on the wallpaper. We'd never greet each other, she'd just get up, faking cheer, and go to the kitchen to fetch a pre-prepped meal tray with two plates of noodles. *Laura, I made us food.*

I keep my phone off; every once in a while I turn it back on again to see if there are any more missed calls from Blanca, but no, she stopped calling. I head out with Antonia to walk along that same plaza where the car would make the turn, trying to rein in my memories. I text Felipe asking if he's home yet.

7

In Esther's box there's a picture from her wedding. It was quick, nothing formal, just before the military coup. They're outside a Civil Registry office in Santiago Centro. She's in a white miniskirt, my father in bell-bottoms. Their friend Toro is standing beside them; they would go into exile with him soon after. There's no family from Michel's side. He'd cut ties with his upper-class pedigree, as he calls it, due to political differences. I made a bad deal! he'd joke when he didn't have the money for child support. My grandmother Nora is pictured on the left, dressed in black as if in mourning. Clinging to her, a peevish boy with slicked-back hair in a three-piece suit: Camilo.

My mother supposedly had no siblings—that is, until her father died when she was a teen. That's when Camilo showed up, a lost son from some affair my grandfather had successfully kept hidden. Camilo knocked on the door when he was ten years old in search of his absent father, planning to ask to live with him, only to stumble upon the news that he'd already died. My grandmother Nora, a saint who always forgave, adopted him and raised him like just another child of her own. But Camilo was not just another child. He'd steal and disappear, and he never managed to graduate from high school. My grandmother Nora suffered through raising him. Then my mother went into exile and lost track of him. When she returned, Camilo knocked on our door and asked for his part of the inheritance from my grandparents. What inheritance? It was hardly two beans to rub together, my mother said to him laughing. So he asked for his part of the house we were living in, and my mother—who was easily guilted—wound up allowing Camilo to live with us until he could get on his feet. Which took him four years.

I'll tell it as I remember it.

To me, Camilo was not my uncle; he was just some guy living in the room at the back of the house who made me uncomfortable. I didn't want him near me. At the same time, he'd make me laugh with the charismatic way he'd poke fun at my mother. That was a skill of his. At times he was such a charmer that you'd forget who he really was, as if he could hit pause on your memory. When my father stopped calling and sending letters from France, Camilo began taking up more and more space in our house, becoming increasingly enmeshed in our lives without us realizing.

I'd come home from school, and it would look like everything had been ransacked—the nightstands pulled open, the clothing rummaged through, it even looked like my diary had been read. Things would disappear from the house: a painting, or the vacuum, never jewelry or anything of value that might cause my mother to kick him out. He'd be gone for days and then return with this electric energy. In an attempt to win back my mother's approval, he'd do it all: he'd make food for ten people, fix the dishwasher—even if it wasn't broken—and wash the stone patio, using laundry detergent, wilting the grass in the suds. With the money my mother would lend him, he'd buy unnecessary things for the house, appliances we never knew how to use, an enormous rug, a tree we had nowhere to plant; then everything would disappear.

During fits of euphoria that he'd mask as affection, he would cover my mouth and crush my nine-year-old body against the armchair, pressing down until he made me cry. It's a game, he'd say, don't exaggerate. I have this image of him running amok through the house, screaming. Perhaps it wasn't quite like that, but it could have been. At that age, children see everything, we feel everything, we notice everything. We're aware. We don't need things to actually happen to see them. We don't have the language or reflective thinking that adults do, but we know the truth because it enters our bodies without filter, whereas adults have all the tools and capabilities but choose not to see. Perhaps Camilo never got to the point of screaming wildly, but that image was a threat that hung over me, like so many others.

My mother dragged Camilo to various psychologists, but he'd never keep up with the sessions. She was trying to put right the *un-put-rightable*—I knew that wasn't a real word, but I got a kick out of using it. My mother got it in her head that capitalism was behind Camilo's imbalance; the emptiness of Chilean society in the nineties had managed to break him, making his lies, manipulations, and drug addiction even worse, she'd say. That sounded to me like something out of a TV show. I was never quite sure she was right about that, because my mother was a bit over the top when it came to the subject. What's more, things were never overt with Camilo; nothing he did was ever that serious. A psychologist told me that Camilo was the identified patient, the one embodying all that was wrong in the family, but that no one wanted to see. Or perhaps it wasn't a psychologist but me as an adult trying to find an explanation on Google for that darkness and euphoria disguised as charm, that constrained violence that he'd subtly release.

Given his drug issues, my mother decided to send Camilo to Cuba. She believed communism could save anyone, but it didn't work out that way. Camilo was the same parasite as always, except farther away. He was living a bourgeois life smack in the middle of the Special Period. He'd spend my mother's money in the supermarkets and stores meant for tourists, while taking advantage of the benefits of communism and the goodwill of my mother's friends. He got a job as a taxi driver and found himself a Cuban woman so he wouldn't be alone. After a year, Esther asked him to come back because she could no longer support his deadbeat life.

When Camilo returned, my mother had received her first cancer diagnosis, and she was very unwell. She'd only eat the soups she'd wearily make for herself; she couldn't stomach anything else. During that time, my home was silent, full of questions about her health that I never dared to ask. Camilo was the same as always. Things would disappear; he would disappear. He'd shut himself in his room with the curtains drawn and let his unwashed dishes pile up beneath his bed. Then he'd reappear, rambling nonstop. In his periods of euphoria there were times he wouldn't sleep. One of those nights, Camilo crawled into my bed and touched my body as I slept; he pressed his body against mine as I, groggy from sleep, tried to push him off me. I woke up afraid. Making excuses, he said that he'd had a nightmare, that he'd confused me with the Cuban woman, that I shouldn't exaggerate, that he didn't know what he was doing. Of course he did. He scurried back to his bed in the darkness like a rat. I didn't say a thing and went back to sleep. The next day at lunch I felt uneasy as the three of us ate our soup. He told us about his confusion, between laughs, leaving out the important details, establishing his truth as mine. And my mother remained silent.

In the months that followed, I reconstructed that memory over and over again, and my suspicion of other nights slowly emerged like when the body of a suicide victim floats to the surface. That same rat-like scurrying repeated various times, repressed in the memories of a little girl who doesn't wake up. Camilo continued disappearing and then returning to the house and I asked my mother, without telling her anything, so as not to sap any more energy from that body, to please never allow him into the house again.

And she understood without needing to ask.

8

Felipe's mother sings the most dreadful, made-up songs to keep Antonia entertained; she bangs the toy drum offbeat as she sings her lyrics that don't quite rhyme. Antonia listens to them, bemused. Without looking at her I know that's the expression on her face: bemusement. I close the door to try to rest. Felipe says I'm overcritical of his mother, of him, of Antonia, of the house too. I've become obsessed with order and cleanliness ever since she was born. When I find things out of place—bibs on the armchair, earbuds dangling off my bookcase, a T-shirt in the kitchen—I break down. So, I choose to clean and organize while Antonia sleeps—the only time I have for myself—and I'm furious at those earbuds that wander off where they don't belong, at my skin that won't shrink back, and at this life that refuses to return to how it was.

Now it's time to play, play, play I hear Felipe's mother sing, and I silently plea for Antonia to cry so I can get her out of there. But my daughter is so bubbly, and she adores her grandmother. I, however, am worn out. I don't talk much, and I don't sleep much. My mind is racing all the time. I try to see myself, but I'm in the middle of a storm, and things are hazy from in here. Of course I'm messing up. I'm making mistakes. That's what mothers do, make mistakes. Their mistakes shape us as human beings; we grow by molding ourselves to them.

Things between me and Felipe, they aren't good—gone is our space to daydream. Our lives are spent surviving our reality, and it is crushing our spirits. Of course things could be different. I seek out support in a group chat for first-time mothers, but they're just as much at their wit's end. They send pictures of poop and voice notes with their babies crying at four o'clock in the morning, and I can't compete with that. The Instagram moms seem to have it all under control. They post pictures of food plated and organized by color and wrap their babies in ancestral fabrics with a perfectly tied knot that leaves their backs hunched, just as Mother Nature intended or something like that.

Seeing those mothers, they seem happy to me.

I hate pediatricians. In the last few months, we've gone to see some ten different doctors. We're looking for non-existent explanations for why life is like this now. It's because Antonia doesn't sleep, which is true; she keeps waking up more and more. Some babies' sleep patterns evolve; our baby's devolves.

Every three hours,
every two,
every one.

I want to believe that she'll sleep one day: all humans sleep. I'll sleep again too, they tell me. The rational part of me understands this, but she is not the mother. The mother is a scared little girl looking for explanations from every pediatrician as to why life is the way it is right now. Nevertheless, I'm happy. I think about Felipe, Antonia, this house, those earbuds that don't even work, while lying in the comfort of this room where I'm supposedly resting, and I know that everything is okay. Why then, when I leave this room, does everything cloud over? It doesn't make sense. Perhaps it's not about Antonia not sleeping, but about something I don't want to see, as one anthroposophic pediatrician put it. You're disconnected from her; try to join her sleep while you nurse her at night. Use it as a sacred time for the two of you. I snapped in response asking if he by any chance had ever breastfed. We went to someone else, a blunt-spoken doctor who didn't mince words. He told us to stop googling crap and to keep her more bundled up; she was waking up from being too cold and just needed to be warmer. You see? Felipe said, and ever since, we've been wrapping her tight. I don't like her getting so warm, so sweaty and flushed; it makes me uncomfortable to see her like that, trapped. I'd rather she be cool, free to move, open to the world. At night, as soon as I can, I furtively remove her layers.

9

During the final months of my pregnancy I was exhausted, and so I scaled back at work, teaching only two courses at the university. I didn't bring home any essays to grade and mostly did oral assessments. That's not what I'm supposed to do, but the department heads are completely oblivious and there were no student complaints on the faculty survey. No engineer considers art history a priority. I'd like to stay at this pace for at least a couple of years, so I can be with Antonia. I want to watch her grow. At the same time, I'm overwhelmed from spending so much time with her.

My mother could never wrap her head around the idea of working less, but she would also say that taking care of people is work, so I manage the guilt. Esther believed that working like a dog kept her strong, independent, free of something, although I just saw her enslaving herself. She'd work full time at the school, and then we'd go home together, where she'd sit in the dining room eating buttered bread, smoking, and grading tests while I ate dinner and did my homework, which she would also go over in detail at the end of the day. *The only thing I can leave to you, Laura, is your education.*

On weekends she couldn't sit still. She'd wash the sheets, hang the sheets to dry, iron the sheets, and I'd water the garden. Then together we'd watch TV. The first time she fell ill, she wanted us to spend more time together. She never said that directly, but she started behaving out of character, like when she pretended we had to leave school early for one of her doctor's appointments so she could take me to Santiago Centro to see La Moneda, the capitol building, and to gaze up at the hillside of Cerro Santa Lucía from the street. When things were at their most difficult, she was docile. She came across as affectionate because she spoke with more of a hush, her body moved less—she didn't have the energy to worry. But she'd also clam up more than usual, which gave me this unending feeling of guilt and uncertainty. What would you like to do? she'd sometimes ask, and I'd say I wanted to go to the movies, or I'd ask her to buy me clothes at the mall, like my friends got to do. She'd arm herself with patience to humor me. She'd wait hunched over in a chair next to the register in the awful department store while I picked out clothes. I chose simple things because, like she'd always say, we weren't there for a fashion show; I didn't want to give her a reason to say it again. We'd head home in a taxi, in silence, stuck in nauseating stop-and-go traffic, and I'd hug my new clothes to my chest with an also unending feeling of emptiness.

10

1998, Playa Santa María del Mar, La Habana.

I'm twelve years old, my mother is in her forties. The picture's a bit blurry. She's looking at me out of the corner of her eye, smiling, and it looks like I've just burst out laughing. Written on the back of the photograph: *Laurita and me.* The stories behind people's faces in childhood photos are a mystery. You see a mother in a bikini, looking young and gorgeous, with the daughter she bore, and although a rift is forming between them, the joy captured in the photo will be the final word—the irrefutable record of their happiness.

I attempt to reconstruct something from the few pictures she has in her box of us together, but the photos leave gaps like black holes.

1998, Plaza de la Revolución, La Habana.

I'm clinging to her worn-out purse strap. We're holding little paper flags, and the girls my age in the crowd are wearing mustard-yellow uniforms. The face of Fidel can be seen from afar on the white canvas, static like a Lego's.

The first time Esther took me to Cuba I was twelve years old; we went to visit her friends from her time in exile. We spent the most time with Alberto and Nadine, the Cuban couple who first welcomed her when she arrived. They were divorced but living together. According to them, finding another place to live was impossible, and it was better to just put up with each other. Given things were tense at their place and Esther didn't want to put them out, we stayed in a hotel next to the Malecón with a lobby full of light and a continental breakfast. There was an old man in a white shirt pressing habanos all day long and a woman singing "Guantanamera" every night in the restaurant. They were there day after day, with the forced joy and enthusiasm of a debut performance, as if they were stuck in a movie on loop. I suppose my mother put up with the theater of it all because she preferred the comfort of amenities; over the years she'd grown used to it. Feeling a bit guilty, as soon as we'd leave the hotel, she'd make a point of behaving as down-to-earth as possible, which most resembled the Cuba inside her.

Alberto and Nadine, like most Cubans, were not permitted to enter the hotel, so we'd meet them outside where they'd be waiting on a little bench near the entrance. During our time in La Habana we did more or less the same thing every day. In the mornings we'd go out with them to see the sights, the muggy wind tousling our hair, and they'd reminisce about a past I wasn't a part of. We'd spend the afternoons in some plaza or swimming at the beach and for lunch we'd eat sandwiches that had something resembling pork in them, which my mother told me I couldn't say no to. Then we'd hop on the "guagua," as they're known in Cuba, and hang out the door of the packed bus on our way to visit other friends. But we only did that twice because my mother grew weary of the two-hour wait; so, ashamed, she hired a Cuban man for a few dollars who'd take us around in his old-fashioned car. In the evenings we'd eat dinner at Nadine and Alberto's and my mother would talk with them into the night. I'd pretend to be asleep on the armchair because I wanted to listen to her, to Esther, to the woman my mother was when I wasn't around. During those conversations they talked about the feeling of camaraderie at the peñas folklóricas organized by the exiles and the empanadas my mother insisted on making, out of nostalgia, even though she'd never been a good cook. They also spoke of the trips to Matanzas to see Nadine's family and a memorable vacation they took to the Isla de la Juventud—its name, the Isle of Youth, always made me laugh—which they swore they'd return to, but never did. She also spoke of my father, with levity, as if she loved him. And they laughed, my mother most of all, like she never did in Chile.

While she was nostalgically living in the Cuba of her memories, I found myself in a Cuba I was struggling to understand. Their way of life was so different from ours in Santiago, and it confused me. I tried to make the island fit with what I'd learned about the Caribbean at school. Over the summer, my classmates would travel to Miami or the Dominican Republic and they'd come back to school tan with braids and with coconut rings to share around. One day, while we were eating fried plantains—there was surely something else on the plate that I didn't want to eat—I asked my mother if I could get my hair braided, like my friends. We're-not-in-that-Caribbean, she said, with such staccato that if she'd written it on a piece of paper, she herself would've used scissors to cut it off at the period. I asked Nadine to convince her—as if it were urgent—and she wound up giving in. We went to her hairdresser, a neighbor who did clients' hair in her bathroom and raised roosters in the yard. She put my hair in forty-four braids (I counted them) and tied them off with bits of thread. I asked if she had any colored beads like I'd seen on my friends, but she had no idea what I was talking about. I laughed, but my mother didn't find it funny. A couple of days later the thread fell out and the braids came loose before I went back to school. I told you! she shouted, laughing. My mother was right: that island was different.

The trip to La Habana triggered my urge to know Esther. I realized I didn't know much about her, besides her silences, her halfhearted scolding, and her wearied tutoring sessions on French spelling, which I never managed to master. In Cuba I saw her as a different woman, freer, with a past, with choices that had nothing to do with the two of us. I came to understand that it was her place in the world: those streets frozen in time where she walked smoking and laughing, her eyes closing at the touch of the wind, her body wet and covered in sand, as if that air carried her far away from me. Far away from everything. Seeing her like that scared me, as if she were growing distant with those memories, as if the island were capable of snatching her away from me. I began to think that being my mother was something that drained her, that if she'd been able to stay in that past, she would have. I wonder if all of us daughters, all of us mothers, have that doubt. Perhaps I never really knew her.

Perhaps she did want to share herself, but we weren't speaking the same language. In any case, it's too late to ask now.

On the last Sunday of our trip, we waited in a long line at a famous ice-cream shop to get an awful strawberry and chocolate ice cream that my mother enjoyed to no end. Then we went to a movie theater called Acapulco to see a movie with Penélope Cruz—I remember because it was the first time I felt attracted to a woman. The night before our trip back to Santiago, she asked me if I'd had a good time. We were in the hotel room, lying down in the queen bed we were sharing, listening, at her insistence, to Fidel giving a speech on TV. Yes, I told her, I had a good time. She took the leap and pulled me into a hug, and I hugged her back. My heart was thundering, from fear and from the strangeness of that embrace. And I cried in silence, trying not to let her see. I like to imagine that she cried too. We fell asleep like that, in that embrace, with Fidel's voice floating into our dreams, in a speech that, the next day, Nadine would tell us had lasted five hours.

When I returned from summer break that March, braidless, my friends asked where I'd traveled to. To Cuba, I said while handing out the Che-adorned key chains my mother had bought for them. I told them about the beach, the old-fashioned movie theater, and the Malecón. It's so different from here, a different way of life, I said, feigning the maturity that comes with travel. Seeing their faces devoid of awe, I made up that Esther had let me drink rum and that I'd met Pablo Milanés, but they didn't know who that was. Since my mother had spent the entire trip longing to move back, I also made up that we might move to La

Habana, that I was sad to leave Chile, but that the people were free and happy there. But how could you move to Cuba, it's full of communists, they said. It hit me that that word was not a label to be proud of, the way my mother was, but instead the most offensive thing you could be called at that school. I felt embarrassed by us and was furious with her for teaching me things that were of no use to me in navigating that world, a world unlike Esther's and that of her past, a world that stood for everything she hated but she had still chosen for me.

A couple of years ago I went back to La Habana with Felipe. We took an eight-hour red eye, but didn't sleep a wink—I spent the whole trip sharing anecdotes, rambling and vague, that attempted to paint a picture of the country he was about to experience. But when we landed the city felt strange. It was different but also the same: the same scent, the same muggy wind, the same man pressing tobacco leaves, and the same guitar being played in the restaurant. The landscape was the same, but also different; she was no longer there, and I was no longer a girl. The streets once empty were filled with cars. There were more small businesses and restaurants, and the US flag was flying above its embassy. It was no longer Fidel's Cuba and, like me, the island seemed to be wandering about, lost like a headless animal. Somewhere in time Esther was still my mother and I her daughter, but that distance between us when I was a girl, death had made it unfathomable.

Nadine and I didn't manage to meet up, she'd moved back to Matanzas. She kept pressing me to take a trip out there, for us to go to Isla de la Juventud, but I couldn't bring myself to make that journey, because it wasn't ours to make. We spent the rest of the trip at a resort in Varadero and did all the touristy things I couldn't do when I was twelve: we ate lobster, swam inside a cave with its crystal-clear waters, and took a picture with a crocodile. I had wanted to go on the trip as a way to remember her, and I wound up doing everything she hated. I couldn't measure up to her; I never knew how. I wanted to feel close to her, share something of Esther with Felipe, but I only managed to further the distance between us. The closest we'd been had already passed, without my knowing it, on that very island, in that embrace, twenty years prior.

11

My therapist says relationships are full of cracks, that they're not these finished, flawless works of art, but are instead these ordinary earthen jugs that have been pieced back together over and over again. The cracks are the mark of a shared bond, she tells me. But how many times can we smash a jug? Leaving it intact is not an option—to do so is akin to living no life at all—but I wonder just how many cracks a jug can bear before it shatters so completely that nothing of substance is left to rebuild.

I think of how I never heard my mother yell; we never fought. I don't know where our cracks were—they were buried deep. Was our jug masquerading as flawless? With Felipe our cracks are everywhere; they're crawling up the walls of this house. The two of us argue and I tidy up the house, the closets; I put everything back in its place time and time again. I play with Antonia, water the grass, and try to keep this vessel afloat, but sometimes I just can't. I lock myself in the bathroom and compulsively scarf down cookies while the shower's running. Antonia wails in Felipe's arms, crying out for me. The bathroom is the only excuse I have to be absent. And when it's over I come out to hug her with all the love I can give, because I'm trying.

Before Antonia was born, we had no idea how easy things were. When I went on prenatal leave, Felipe would duck out of work sometimes so we could spend the afternoon together; we'd buy ice cream in the plaza, arms slung around each other, and sit chatting about our anxieties around our impending parenthood. Now, not a day goes by without mutual hatred. Every time Antonia wakes up crying—six times a night—we yell at each other while trying to figure out what to do. Felipe thinks it's my fault Antonia doesn't sleep because every time she cries, I nurse her. He says I don't give him the space to learn how to soothe her and her the space to get used to not being with me. But he doesn't get that this is the whole point. This time is for me and Antonia. We'll never have this again, and even if I complain of how overwhelmed I am, I don't want to be apart from her. During our most recent fight, Felipe stood in the doorway blocking me from going in to her while she was hysterically crying in her room. Enough, you're not going in. I did what I could to push him out of the way and locked myself in her room. I tried calming her down, but we were both worked up. We fell asleep in the rocking chair, Antonia in my arms, and I awoke to Felipe trying to break in—apparently Antonia had been crying for some time. He'd been yelling through the door to me, afraid, asking if we were okay, getting no response. I'd passed out from exhaustion. I couldn't even hear her crying in my arms. What the hell is wrong with you? he screamed. I tried to explain, but I was confused and panicked by my own behavior. It was the first time I felt unfit to care for her. Felipe grabbed Antonia, and I let them go. I sat there terrified, breathless. Later he brought her back, as if offering a truce, and the three of us went to sleep. When we all woke up at six, like we did every day, we shouted the same words as always and slammed doors just as always. This time, I told Felipe that I needed my space with Antonia, and I asked him, perhaps a bit dramatically, not to come back.

I wonder if what we've built, with these cracks that are forming—this thing Felipe and I have created—is fracturing because that's what happens to love when you have children; it's how the ceramic looks and that's okay, because there's no such thing as a jug untouched ... or perhaps the therapist is just trying to make me feel better because her job would be meaningless otherwise.

12

A taxi pulls up and I jump in, impatient; it has that pine tree scent and the reggaeton turned up on the radio. Drop us at the corner of Marín and Salvador, Blanca yells to the driver—still annoyed with me—but first I want to make a stop to buy some cigarettes. She then asks him to lower the volume as she rolls down the window, wearing that trademark expression of hers where she scrunches her face in disdain.

After months of not going out, I'm leaving Antonia with Felipe's mother for the first time. She's been insisting—relentlessly, since she was born—on spending the night with her at some point. I know you two had a fight, she said walking in, but I told her I'd rather not talk about it. Then she pulled out a package wrapped in gift wrap recycled from Christmas: a giant Peppa Pig bag with a can of formula inside. She's intent on proving my milk doesn't fill Antonia up and that that's why she wakes up so often throughout the night. I told her, with whatever patience I could muster, that I'd spent the last week pumping to have enough milk for today, so please only give her what I pumped. I hid the can behind the dishes—she'll find it, no doubt—and ran out to the taxi to make the most of the four hours I have before Antonia realizes I'm not there.

The corner of Marín and Salvador is where my friend Nico has his apartment. It's old, spacious, and decorated, with everything in its place, like in a magazine. Blanca's sitting in an art deco armchair, as if she were a painting, with her back straight and a glass of wine in her hand, meanwhile I slouch smoking mar-iguana—as my mother always called it—perfecting the hump I've been working on since 1986. We toast to the end of my cohabitation, which is what they're jokingly calling my fight with Felipe, and I laugh through my tears. Soon after, a young woman shows up: Daniela, the star in one of the movies repped by Blanca's agency. Part of Blanca's job is to parade her around. Don't worry, she's chill, Blanca says when she notes my discomfort. She couldn't be a day over twenty-five with her dollface and dyed pink hair. She takes out her phone to show the trailer for her movie, so Nico and I can figure out who she is, but we have no idea. Regardless we offer the expected praise, and she plays it off, shaking her head in feigned humility.

Nico and I used to date back in our university days; he was my TA for Contemporary Art. My friends would refer to him as El Frida Kahlo, poking fun at his mother. She was an artist who'd made a small fortune in the aughts plagiarizing Mexican folk art that she'd sell for exorbitant prices to the Chilean "red set" with their champagne socialism. Nico and I were together for a couple of years, never in love, always friends. He also went out with Blanca when I introduced them, but things never really caught on because, according to her, he was bad in bed. Right now he's going on about how sex is overrated, and I nod in agreement because I'm a celibate mother, but also because these days I don't do much pushing back, it drains too much of my life force. Traditional Chinese medicine tells me that a considerable part of your life force is inherited from your parents. I don't know about my father's life force because I so rarely see him and don't have it in me to ask. As for my mother, by the time she had me, she hardly had any left, so I probably got mine from her. While pregnant I tried some Eastern methods I'd heard about to help myself, like eating egg drop soup and going for acupuncture, but I've given up on that now and am back to being passive, my comfort zone. When you're lacking in life force it impacts libido, I want to tell Nico, and that he should eat more egg drop soup, but he wouldn't understand and I'm in no condition right now to be explaining these things to people. I can't follow the conversation; all I can do is focus on the image of Blanca, Nico, and me sitting here, friends now for years, the same but older, and recall the life we once lived while young, a life to which we can never return.

These days when Felipe comes over he's in and out, watching Antonia in the evenings after work and then leaving. He's sleeping at his mother's or somewhere else; I don't know and don't ask. I hardly speak to him. Our attempts to talk always end in shouting. Sometimes I'm relieved he's not here. I don't have the brainpower or energy to make up or bicker about anything, and bickering with Felipe is like having a full-on trial in court. Objection; no further questions. Perhaps this space we're taking is the best thing for the three of us right now.

I head to the guest bathroom near the front door of Nico's apartment. I take a look at myself in the mirror, breathe, and open the medicine cabinet. Inside I find tissues, mints, condoms—it's like a hotel. Nico's neuroticism is so off-putting to me. There's a mini perfume bottle, too. I take a snorting whiff of it to see if I pass out, and I spill it all over myself. I turn on the faucet to wash my shirt and wind up soaked. Grabbing some toilet paper, I try to blot my shirt dry, and it leaves behind a white papery fuzz on the black fabric. I stare at the fuzz. I shouldn't have smoked. Using a new bar of soap, I go to wash my hands, but it slips out of my grip and falls into the toilet. I unroll a long piece of toilet paper to fish it out, manage to get it, but then the toilet paper gets stuck to the soap, so I give up and throw it all out in the little trash can. I'm exhausted. I pee in that tiny bathroom. The wall in front of me is full of artwork that features musicians staring straight at me. A bald Britney Spears looks me directly in the eyes, playing at being my reflection. I get lost in thought, going over the timeline of my story with Felipe, and see my shadow from outside myself, as if observing everything I'm doing wrong without realizing it. I land on exactly why I threw him out, then forget, like when you dream, and it all fades from your mind as you wake. I walk out of the bathroom holding my phone with my jaw clenched; the pink-haired girl is out on the balcony singing while a neighbor yells at her to shut up. Nico asks if I'm okay.

"I want to go home," I tell him.

"OK, dry that shirt off, I'll call you a taxi. Just don't text Felipe."

"I already did."

"What did you say?"

"That I can't do this, that I don't want to be a mom."

I munch on some cake wrapped in a paper towel; Nico gave it to me so I'd have something in my stomach as I headed back—it tastes metallic. I try to keep track of where the car is going by watching the map, but my eyes keep closing and my body's lurching around. I delete the text I sent Felipe and then google what mar-iguana in my milk can do to Antonia. Horrible things show up in the results. Then I scroll through the pink-haired girl's Instagram, but her dollface is nowhere to be found; she only posts these conceptual photos that I don't understand. When we pull up to my house I get out, drowsy. I try to open the door without making a sound, but the streetlight is out, and I can't find the keyhole. I creep slowly up the wooden stairs, trying not to let the floorboards creak. The climb feels eternal, as if I were falling asleep on every step. In the hallway, barefoot, I walk by Antonia's room, mine when I was a girl, and hear Felipe's mother in there snoring with her. I don't peek inside; I pass right on by, hurrying my pace. When I get to our bed, I'm reminded it's real—another night Felipe didn't come home to sleep.

At nine in the morning I wake from the dead, and the house is steeped in silence. My mouth is pale and dry, and my breath is atrocious. I jump up, panicked, and run through the house in search of Antonia. I find her sitting quietly in her chair while Felipe's mother washes a bottle. She slept right through! she yells, and Antonia cries when she sees me. My breasts are engorged, rock-hard and burning, and I nurse her with relief. I feel indecent beneath her gaze as she reaches out that tiny hand to brush my skin.

"I topped her off with a little formula and she passed right out!"

13

He was right there with me when I took the pregnancy test, in the bathroom of our apartment at the time. Felipe didn't wait outside the door like they do in the movies; he plopped right down in front of me on those cold bathroom tiles while I peed on the stick—he always took the whole "we're in this together" thing seriously. We waited for the result, and when we saw the positive line he gave me a nervous look and I lay down on the floor surprised by a feeling I didn't expect to feel. I'd thought seeing a positive would be a catastrophe, but it wasn't turning out that way. I was tempted to freak out, to say to Felipe that this can't be happening, but, as always in our story, I decided to let go, letting myself free-fall while staring at the ceiling that was rusting out from the humidity, feeling time slow without a thought as to whether or not this was the right path. I was overcome with this feeling of understanding everything, a gift born of learning I had a zygote—as Felipe was calling it—in my uterus. So, when he asked me, with his nineteenth-century formality, if I wanted to do this, I was suddenly hit with the urge to put down roots together, the three of us.

Felipe and I met during my first few weeks as a full professor at the university, an opportunity I'd been waiting on for years while cobbling together a schedule of the occasional university class alongside teaching at a Legionaries of Christ Catholic school. I'd cross the city dressed bleakly in gray, per the dress code, to teach art to a class of bleak-looking girls. Then I'd race over to the university dressed the same way. Felipe, before knowing me, thought I was Mormon. When I was finally able to shake off the Catholic school, we ran into each other in the shared space for those of us who were office-less. And in those impersonal cubicles that we'd pass off as our own, Felipe and I would sit together and grade essays. Over lunches with fellow professors he'd listen to me complain about the engineering students and, with that tone of his that could make anything sound important, he'd talk to me about books and anime. At the time, I was interested in men who were full-bloodedly masculine, and Felipe was feather-like—scrawny, anemically calm. But I told myself: don't question it. That uncomplicated friendship, a bit boring at times but consistent, was good for me.

Every once in a while, I'd expect that simplicity between us to disappear after a long bout of silence or an awkward text exchange. Dejected, I'd be afraid of our bond growing strained, that we'd stop talking for no reason, because up until then that's what most of my relationships had been like. The last ten years of my life had gone like this: I'd move from one shared apartment to another, go on trips to find myself with nothing to show for it—it was a series of breakups that left me feeling warworn. So whenever I got the sense that our relationship could fall apart too, I'd pull back, go lukewarm.

But the next day there he'd be, right there in the cafeteria.

The slow passing of days in which nothing much happened knit something strong between us. And by the time we got together, all my doubts had vanished. We were always carried forward by this wonderful inertia, as if we blindly trusted whoever was slowly pulling along our little cart. But that smooth progress, which had been our North Star, was now impossible to maintain, because when Antonia arrived, things became undeniably real. And in undeniably adult life we all get hit with what's undeniably real, and we weren't about to be the exception.

14

2001, Santiago

Joyeux Anniversaire, Laurita

Seated around a table in a restaurant, under the glare of a flash that made the picture come out darker, the three of us look happy. Michel euphoric, Esther with her eyes closed, and me dressed in the fluorescent clothes of the times. You smile like a crocodile, Michel would say to me after he developed it.

There was a time when my father wanted to do things right, or better than he'd done them since we parted ways in France. He decided that my fifteenth birthday was an important one and made a special trip to celebrate it. He spent several weeks with us during which he insisted we go out for fun, hurriedly trying to get caught up. He introduced me to his longtime friends, who spoke of him with admiration, as if he were a hero. We rode Santiago's aerial cable car and took a bus to the coast to visit the Litoral de los Poetas, where he showed me the house of a writer I'd never read. That's where he took his life, in that stairwell, he told me.

On the night of my birthday, we went out to eat with my mother and he gave me an antique jewelry box. Admittedly I did come up short on the jewelry, he said, and we both laughed. Throughout his entire stay Michel and Esther made an effort to skirt around any tension between them, even though it was always there, thrumming in the background. Even so, in the photo the waiter took of us, they managed not to show it.

Michel let me drink two Vaina cocktails; *laisse-la*, he said to my mother in a commanding tone. By the end of the night, I was drunk. Michel talked nonstop the whole way back so Esther wouldn't realize. And when she was finally asleep in her bed, Michel stood watch for me at the bathroom door, laughing. Now please don't go telling her, he said. Then we sprawled out on the couch to watch whatever was on and fell asleep—according to him, my mouth was wide open.

I saw him off at the airport with a long hug and my mother gave him a quick pat on the shoulder. That was the last time the three of us would be together. Months later he sent me the photo from that night. Although we never discussed it, I think all of us thought of that picture as a nice memory.

15

The neighbor rang the doorbell yet again while I was trying to put Antonia down for a nap. I had her resting in my arms with her eyes closed, but her little body remained alert to respond to any sign of me setting her down. Leaning over to lay her in the crib, praying she wouldn't wake so I could rest for an hour, the doorbell rang—the doorbell that I had insisted we install. Her eyes flew open and that was the end of that. I gripped her, squeezing with rage, growling like an animal. Frightened, she looked up at me, but daughters forgive. I walked outside, holding Antonia, to see if it was something urgent, but that's never the case.

Why does that baby cry so much, deary? I hear the neighbor say, and I absently answer her with an I-don't-know. She invites us over to her house, and I'm not opposed to following her. Her backyard doesn't look like ours: the grass is a divot-less carpet and the pittosporum shrub flanking the entry gate has been shaped into a perfect sphere—unlike ours, which casts a shadow over everything. The hydrangeas run neatly along the small stone path leading back to the patio. We take a seat beneath the shadow of an orange tree as I nurse, and the neighbor covers my breasts with the burp cloth, but I take it off. We're facing a gorgeous yet unassuming display of bougainvillea that adorns the wall between the two houses. I don't recall ever having been here before, but I do recall that Esther would always greet the neighbor warmly when they were both out on the front sidewalk sweeping or watering. I'm unaware of whether she knows that Esther was my mother, and I don't feel like having that conversation. Behind me I notice a small pomegranate tree shrouded in shadow, perhaps the only sad-looking tree in here. I touch it in sympathy. That's why I called on you, she says; your maqui tree is blocking all the light from reaching this poor pomegranate tree, and it won't bear fruit. The neighbor's son—who, as his mother tells it, wound up a confirmed bachelor—joins the conversation to show me a number of tools and a long ladder. I have everything I need to trim it, he says. I move Antonia to my other breast on purpose, to make him uncomfortable, and then gaze up at the branches of our maqui that's reaching with its monstrous arms into this garden full of light. I'd never questioned its size before. Its gigantic branches have created something of a roof over their patio which to me is beautiful. It's practically a weed, says the neighbor's son, but no, no it's not. It's a native tree, my mother would always say, and it can do what it wants with its space. It sprouted naturally from the earth, even before these houses were built, and has more of a right to the land here than we do. I thank him and say that I'll tell Felipe to trim it, but I won't, just like my mother never did, and the neighbor knows it. Nature, you have to guide it, deary, she says; you can't just let it go like that. I don't answer, giving it some thought. Antonia has fallen asleep at my breast, so that's how I carry her back, and the neighbor escorts us for fear of something I don't understand.

16

October 2003, Santiago

The grayish light of the afternoon. An impromptu table spread of coffee and cookies. Ten people seated in classroom chairs, the finish on them peeling. Esther appears gaunt with her blackened teeth and her collarbone cast in shadows; even so, she has a peaceful look about her.

This photo, the last one of us together, was printed out by her friends from her political party, and she'd tucked it away alongside the others. They'd thrown her a malón, as her generation called them, to raise money for her final treatment, in a community center in Macul. At the party there was brief talk of her health, as if she were getting better, and then, over the pisco her friends insisted on opening, they reminisced about marches, meetings, and those who had died. She nodded along, chatted, and offered the occasional smile, although she was clearly tired. I paid close attention to those trips down memory lane, little scraps from images I was piecing together to discover the Esther she no longer was. But those conversations, full of gaps and silences, only made the image of her face seem even more out of focus to me. There were so many times I could've asked more about her past, but I was a coward and ran out of time, afraid she'd suddenly shut the door in my face. So instead, I was left with something of a cliché postcard of that era which, in the end, told me nothing about who she was.

On our way home we took the route we always did, walking past the bakery and the dog that always barked at us, crossing the road when we saw someone strange. She gazed up at the cherry trees in bloom and seemed resigned, but strong in her own right, which made me feel that I should act like I felt that way too. She spoke of practical things, and also told me, as if convincing herself, while squeezing my hand and avoiding my eyes: I'm going to be okay.

17

It's not a tumor; it's two tumors. My mother was always a bit evasive with her words. She'd never use many, just the ones she thought she needed, unaware of how her silence was shaping my own. *There's another one in my stomach, Laura, and the doctor says the outlook isn't good.* She was levelheaded, discreet, and elegant in her own way, but also hard to read, melancholy, and absent. *I'm supposed to restart chemo next week, but I'm not going to.* I never really knew how to talk to her; even about the things I had most clarity on, I never knew how to put them into words for her. *There's no point, I've already gone through this countless times, I know how it goes.* I'd always avoided those moments, the need to have honest conversations with her, fearing what she had to say to me, or rather, what she wouldn't say. *I'm tired, Laura, I don't want to fight it anymore.* I'd never met another woman whose silence was as powerful as hers. *I won't tell you that I'm going to be okay, because I won't be, that's the truth.* So, when she did talk to me, when she spoke with me like that, looking right at me, the earth seemed to rumble, shaking the foundation of my world. *We need to get my affairs in order.* That night she called me to her room. *I need you to hold it together, to be practical.* I sat at the foot of her bed, blocking the TV. *As for school and university, it's all taken care of; I have insurance, and you'll have everything you need.* I never knew what to make of that calm demeanor. *This house is yours; do you know how many people don't have a place to live? You have a house, and you have your things, and you're going to be fine, don't cry.* Again, I'll be unfair in my thoughts: this was not the fortitude her friends would speak of at the funeral. *And don't worry about me, because I'm at peace.* This was a desire for death. *I talked to your father and filled him in; he's going to help you.* As if that news, delivered from the serenity of her bed, with the volume turned down low on the TV and the cats taking up all the space on the empty half of the mattress, freed her from something. *Michel has his issues, but he's no weón; he'll be there. In his own way, but he'll be there for you.* As if she were finally allowed to fall, unburdened, and float untethered, risk free. *Remember how when you were a little girl you never wanted to go in the water? What would I always tell you?* Fearless, carefree, her body drifting like foam, undaunted by the water's violence. *When there's a big wave coming don't try to avoid it, remember? If you do, it'll really throw you around. Instead, dive under and hold your breath until it passes.*

But I have always been afraid of the sea.

Everything I'm saying here is likely an exaggeration or an invention of my memory. Our mothers are not what we believe them to be; our idea of them is just a character we've created for our own convenience, to survive, to keep ourselves going or to recount our own story. My mother was a woman like any other, which is to say, she was a thousand different women. Her colleagues from work, her friends from exile, and my own father would recall her composure as her most noble trait. They wouldn't be so tactless as to tarnish the memory of her calm with my uncharitable version of this story. But this is my memory; it belongs to me, and I have a right to do with it as I please, even if it destroys her. It's possible she said all those things to me or none of them, but it doesn't matter, my memory of that conversation would perhaps be the same, because, for not having said enough to me, I would always have had to fill in those spaces with my own words. *This won't be the first or the last time that everything falls apart for you, Laura.*

And that's how things were between us, always.

18

Our last New Year's Eve, just days before Esther died, we had dinner together in her hospital room. She only managed to get down a few bites, then we shared a feeble embrace before midnight and the nurse suggested we let her rest. I didn't want to spend the night there, so I slipped into the bathroom to get ready to go out and then left to meet up with Blanca for a party in Santiago Centro. It was at an old, ramshackle house. Blanca was wearing a blazer with a plunging neckline and her hair was pulled back; she looked flawless, beautiful. I was in a black dress I'd picked up for cheap on Calle Banderas that was turning out to be shorter than I'd thought. My skinny legs made me look like a little girl, but back then looking like a little girl was comfortable for me. I was unaware of how trapped I was in that body; I saw no need to break free from that childish image.

I remember that night like this:

I've just turned eighteen. I'm smoking, standing in the middle of the dance floor and looking for Jake, a guy I chat with on MSN. Blanca chats with him too—it's practically the same snobby conversation about music and movies. The difference being that Blanca can keep up with him and I have to google things to make it look like I can. Blanca has more of a shot with Jake in real life, but that night we do a coin toss. It comes up heads and Blanca called tails, so she gives me the go-ahead to try and make a move.

Jake has narrow eyes, that haircut where it's long in the back, and a three-day shadow on his face that was all the rage at the time. He's a good deal older than us and lives in Chicago but spends long spells in Chile. Everyone knows he's the son of a right-wing politician, but he never brings it up: he's embarrassed by it. His screen name on MSN is Jake, just Jake; his name is actually pronounced "yake" not "ha-keh," which is how I was saying it in Spanish. Fortunately, Blanca corrected me before meeting him in person. If my mother had known that I was after the son of that facho recalcitrante, as she was apt to call any pig-headed fascist, she would've stopped talking to me for a few days, because she was like that, serious about those kinds of things. She would've asked me if I was, by any chance, unaware of what she'd had to live through. At any rate, my mother had nothing to worry about; Jake was just a fantasy. The Jakes of the world didn't go out with girls like me, they just talked to us to feed their egos.

At the party everyone is beautiful and knows each other, and they're all walking around like they're looking for something. My Calle Banderas dress and I are invisible.

Besides Blanca and Jake, the only other person I know is Romi, from school, who invited us to the party. She wears her hair styled short, like Mia Farrow. Pretty and insufferable, she has a knack for saying hurtful things wrapped up in kind words, like how it feels to bite into a chocolate bonbon and hit that nasty maraschino cherry. I never understood why Blanca was friends with her—they had nothing in common. Romi has a boyfriend in France, she met him during a high school exchange program, and it's all she talks about. While Romi is regaling Blanca with stories of life in Paris—because she would never talk directly to me—I cut in to find out if she's hooked us up with what we asked for. Romi leads us into the kitchen and hands us each a little baggy.

"It's all in there but take it slow, I don't know how strong they are."

Blanca tucks the baggy in with her cigarettes; she won't be trying any that night. I, however, break off a quarter pill and slip it into my mouth. It's dark and cold in that abandoned house. The place belongs to the family of someone at the party but it's soon to be demolished to make room for a new building. The architecture is striking, intimidating. It gives me mala espina, Esther would say; bad vibes indeed. She could see the energy around people, houses, situations, and she was never wrong—well, sometimes she was. And she'd always tell me that I got that intuition from her, that I'm like Persephone, that I can see in the darkness. But that night I don't listen—to my mother or that darkness.

A short guy with an arrogant air, a high-pitched voice, and Napoleonic energy strolls over to chat Blanca up. He claims to know us from school, but his face doesn't ring a bell. Growing weary of him, Blanca mentions diplomatically that her boyfriend must be around here somewhere waiting for her. She waves at some blond guy she's never met, who waves back confused, and walks over to him. I follow, invisible.

"Sorry, I was just trying to get out from under that wet blanket."

"Claudio," he says, playfully extending his hand to Blanca, "but people call me Mono." She offers her hand in return, wrist limp like a princess.

I place my hand lightly on Blanca's arm to give her a heads-up that I'm about to make myself scarce, and she gives it a squeeze to let me know she's good. I pour myself a pisco and soda in a disposable cup and start wandering around looking for Jake. The "dance floor" is a partially crumbling interior patio where the DJ has his turntable sitting on a door that's laid horizontally across a pair of sawhorses. I'm freezing and I shiver, my jaw tense; the pill isn't making me any happier. I spot Jake standing next to a large column, but he hasn't seen me. There's this red flashing light sweeping around the room that keeps hitting me in the eyes, clouding my vision, and every time I blink, he's with another girl. Romi comes up to me.

"Has it hit you yet?"

"My body feels so stiff."

"Weird, I feel great," she says laughing. "Maybe they gave you something else. I wound up having to get yours and Blanca's from some other guy."

The bitter cherry in that sweet bite. I shrug Romi off and the house suddenly feels packed. I see Blanca and Mono talking, and they're having a good time. Later they'll leave the party together, walking toward his house. He'll say he had a great time getting to know her and Blanca will laugh, then ask if he's seeing anyone. He'll say no. When he throws himself at her for a kiss Blanca will say she isn't in the mood and Mono will love this. They'll have an easy conversation, something I'd yet to experience with a man, and Blanca will recount the details, blow by blow, when she calls me the next day, while I pace around the plaza feeling miserable. But at the moment I'm at that party jam-packed with zombies from Santiago's upper-class neighborhoods. I'm dancing next to the makeshift table where the DJ's providing the soundtrack for that ramshackle house. As I dance, I hear the walls crumbling, the floor cracking. I move to the music while taking in the dilated eyes and nervous jaws of those who drift over every now and then to dance with me. As I move, I imagine I'm visiting the underworld, like Persephone; it's an eternal party where I'll never find anything. I move as if shaking off my mother's voice, which reminds me of what I should not be.

I find myself in line for the bathroom and scan the area for Jake. I'm cold; I don't have a jacket with me because it's summer and I didn't feel like carrying one around. It's my turn to go in. The bathroom light is red, the floor is wet, and there's no toilet paper. I take a long moment to stare at myself closely in the mirror. Someone knocks on the door, but I don't respond. I pull out the baggy and throw back another quarter pill, to see if it works, and then slurp up what's left of my pisco. When I open the door, I'm hit with disgusted glares from the women, older than me, who are standing there waiting. I spot Jake, who gives me a smile, jumps the line, and walks into the bathroom with me.

"Where have *you* been?" he says, locking us in. The women outside bang on the door, furious.

"I've been looking for you," I say.

I take out the remaining half pill and put it in my mouth. While I'm in that bathroom, Blanca's arriving at Mono's house. She takes off her heels at the door, her feet covered in blisters from walking so much; she limped the final ten blocks. Mono tries to carry her in, but Blanca refuses, to protect her dignity, she'll tell me the next day.

There are six scenes.

The cast of red light on Jake's face. A taxi. A cold hand fishing beneath my dress. Teeth slamming into my face. A dried-out potted plant falling to the floor and rolling zigzag down a dark hallway. Jake flipping me face down on a bed.

The apartment is gigantic, though sparsely furnished with just an armchair, a corner table covered in dirty glasses, a Persian rug, and a bicycle. Blanca's told me that Jake is one of those faux-poor rich kids, but this is just dingy. I wake up in a large white bed that sits on the floor, like those Japanese floor mattresses. I rummage around for my dress in a mountain of black clothes to no avail. I throw on a T-shirt that smells like armpit. My underwear's tangled up in the sheets. I run to the bathroom so he doesn't wake up, and I shut the door too loudly.

"Coffee?" Jake yells from the bedroom.

"Sure," I yell back.

The bathroom is old and yellowed with a big open window overlooking a sun-filled patio for hanging clothes out to dry, where water drips down from the apartments above—the sweat from all those lives up there. I brush my teeth using toothpaste on my finger and wind up completely soaked. Looking down at the sink I realize it's cracked in half.

"The sink's broken!" Jake yells from the kitchen.

I flash back to the crumbling bricks of last night's underworld and feel like everything is falling apart. I look in the mirror and touch my neck; it's stiff. There's a purple and black bruise that hurts to the touch. My vagina is burning.

"Jake, never mind about the coffee … I have a family lunch."

"Everything okay?" he asks, walking into the bedroom wearing a blue sweatsuit that reminds me of school. I shiver.

"Yeah, totally, I just have to get going to give my mom her New Year's hug."

Jake hands me my dress from where it was lying splayed out on the floor. I throw it on hurriedly, so he won't see my body, and head quickly out the door. He calls after me that it was a pleasure, wachita, and that last word—which makes my skin crawl—makes me feel like I'm falling down an elevator shaft that runs from my purpled neck to my roiling stomach. It's the last time we'll ever see each other.

I walk. It's January first and there's no one out, just an old man walking his poodle. I pull down at the hem of my dress when he passes by. My cellphone rings; it's Blanca. When I hear her voice, I hang up, pretending my phone went dead. I get home after riding the empty metro nine stops and run upstairs to my room to change. I realize I left the cats trapped inside; one of them pooped on the small balcony, which is really more of a place to put your feet to make yourself feel like you're going out somewhere. I step outside, next to the poop, and try to breathe, but I can't get any air down. My mind goes to my childhood and Camilo. I don't ever want anything to enter me again.

I run to the hospital afraid she may already be gone. The nurse has her earbuds in, listening to music. My mother is sleeping with chapped lips and labored breath. I curl up in a ball at the foot of her bed and use my hands to cover that ballooning purple cloud on my neck; it's like a brewing storm.

And it explodes.

19

When we moved into this house, Felipe planted grass in the front yard, beneath the magnolia tree. Today I lay Antonia down for a nap on a blanket in its shadow, joining her myself as if to sleep. As I rest, my eyes fluttering open and shut, the daylight grows dimmer. I avoid looking up at the sky because I hear it can burn your retina. For the last eclipse Felipe's mother came over for lunch, and she and Felipe went outside to watch with the neighbors. They all took turns using the protective glasses, and then the neighbors invited them to toast the event with champagne. I didn't want to go out. I was nine months pregnant, holed up in the house, and I didn't want the eclipse to be over me. I was uneasy about exposing my body to any risks and at the time it seemed risky to me, because Esther believed an eclipse could lead to blotches on the baby.

But today I don't have that fear. The eclipse doesn't interest me much and, in fact, I'd forgotten it was happening. It catches us by surprise as we rest on the freshly replanted grass, plush as a new rug that will probably soon lose its pureness of color, its perfect texture. In a few months' time, the grass will dry out again, starved for light. I know because my mother would also try to keep up with it, reseeding every winter. I didn't mention that to Felipe—so he wouldn't lose hope. But none of that matters; there's grass here today, and it holds us in that darkening silence. Little moon-shaped shadows appear on the driveway pavers. I don't pay them much mind, but I'll later hear they were thought to be one of the eclipse's most beautiful phenomena; they were just shadows to me. The neighbors take to the streets shouting enthusiastically, and I hide so they don't invite me out. I wrap my arm around Antonia and snuggle up to her, breathing in her sweet little neck. I don't want to watch the eclipse; it makes me sad. I'm overcome by this strange perception of time, a duplicity of the present or a simultaneity of all the presents we've experienced together, Antonia and I, my mother and I, in this house.

The light continues growing dimmer, and Antonia rests. It won't go completely dark; totality will occur in a region further north, and people from the city made a special trip up there to see it. Those seaside resorts must be teeming with people looking up at the sky right now. When it's over, the beaches and restaurants will be overrun, and the narrow roads, built for tranquility, will be flooded with cars and noise. Here the light grows soft, like at sunset. Antonia wakes and begins to cry, perhaps out of fear. I understand that jolt of panic when the light begins to fade. Babies and their bodies are sensitive to these changes, the truths that emerge in the darkness. And this semi-darkness, this tepidity of shadows, this timid yet startling night, causes me panic too, and I wish that I could cry like her. I'm suddenly hit with this premonition that time will never be as it was before. When I was a girl, a couple of decades was an eternity, an entire lifetime, something so far-off when I'd be someone I couldn't even imagine—someone like my mother, a serious person, uncomfortable in her body. That couple of decades is today. Since Antonia was born, time seems to have morphed. Weeks have two days: Mondays and Fridays. Then there's a Sunday when, for a few hours, life pauses for a bit, like how trains slow through a station where they won't make a stop. This train won't be stopping anywhere ever again except at its final destination. And through the window I'll be looking out at a landscape growing ever drier. Antonia will stay green, and the memory of my mother will blur with the speed of time, drying out, growing arid, withered.

20

I leave Antonia with Felipe at his mother's house and then head out with Nico to a birthday for Daniela, the pink-haired actress, Blanca's friend. It's at a Chinese restaurant in Santiago Centro, a windowless basement lit only by red-shaded lamps and a couple of fish tanks. There are fifteen people gathered around a table; there's no room for us, and no one acknowledges our arrival but Blanca, who waves from afar. The waiter brings over two extra chairs, but we're still floating outside the circle. We order spring rolls, and they're set down at the very corner of the table, nearly falling off the edge. Nico stains his shirt with soy sauce trying to eat one over his lap.

It's a trendy restaurant where they filmed a scene for Daniela's movie. Our presence here is performative, because that's another part of Blanca's job: curating seemingly candid scenes and posting them on social media. Blanca likes to invite me and Nico to these parties, as if she were doing us a favor by opening this other world to us, although we came more because we wouldn't know where else to go; the last of our youth has now lost touch with the present. All the girls here are dressed like Daniela; she's sitting next to us, wearing oversized clothes that look like they could belong to a boyfriend—apparently the trend. She greets us more warmly than we deserve. I don't recognize anyone else. When we finish eating, a waiter comes by to hand out fortune cookies. Blanca suggests we go around and take turns reading our fortunes aloud. Nico ducks out to the bathroom before it's his turn because he doesn't like games. My fortune says: *Love is closer than you think*, but I don't read it out because I'm embarrassed. I make up a different one, one my mother once got when we ordered Chinese food—which we did quite often—and that she'd always say to me jokingly when I didn't want to get up to look for something: *You're in the perfect place to get there from here.*

No one sings happy birthday.

After we finally settle on how to split the check, Daniela suggests we head to her place to continue the party, with other *amigues*, she says. She lives in a building a few blocks away. Almost no one lives there, just a neighbor here and there, the rest of it is filled with law offices and electronics stores. Nico lets out a howl to test the emptiness, but *ningune*—no one, that is—finds it funny.

The apartment is small. All it has is a computer on a table in the living room and one of those sleeper mattress chairs on the floor. She has a fake plant and a neon light in the shape of a heart. I think of how Daniela is like the character she plays in her movie— even though I've only seen the trailer she showed us—with its slow plot about a way of life that's currently of no interest to me. The kitchen is tiny; it hardly fits a single person. None of the glasses are clean, so we drink out of mugs. When more of Daniela's friends arrive, more twenty-somethings, we make room by sitting jammed together on the floor. Nico looks uncomfortable, like he doesn't know what he's doing here. I feel the same way, but at least my age difference isn't as obvious, I want to believe. After smoking up, someone turns off the lights with an enthusiastic shriek.

Daniela talks to me, the words tumbling out, about the movie, her festival tours, politics, the marches, all of it jumbled up, as if hurried for time. She doesn't ask me a thing, and that's okay with me. I'm silent like a woman in a bunker, a cloistered nun, or a little girl surrounded by adults. I realize I'm on a different planet; over the last few months I lost track of the more than ten years between us. I text Felipe to ask how they're doing, and he answers with a curt: *all good*. Daniela tries to close the gap between us, but I feel like I reek of soy sauce and cabbage, so I pull away. She removes her oversized jacket, and I take note of her flat stomach next to my heavy body. I try to recall what it was like to be like that, to be that way in the world, engaged in the present, full of words, with a body that's light and free of burdens. I dance with her for a bit, in the dimness of the light from the street, and I think of how beautiful her youth is. She leans toward me, and I panic. Blanca, seated next to the neon heart, sees my face and, because she knows it, laughs. She signals to me that she's heading out.

I tell Daniela that I need to use the bathroom, but instead I go grab my purse from her room, which is nothing but an unmade bed, a nightstand with books, and some embroidered feminist slogans that I once believed in too. Nico and Blanca easily slip away and, since the front door is right next to the guest bathroom, we all leave together with no one the wiser. We run down the stairs, our steps echoing. The front gate slams shut behind us, and we sit down on the sidewalk.

"What's going on with you?" Blanca asks.

"I don't know."

"Do you want me to bring you home?"

"No."

We smoke in silence, waiting out the sixteen minutes for the Uber to arrive. They insist on me leaving with them, but they realize I don't want to, and they decide to let it go. As soon as the car turns the corner, I ring the bell to go back inside; someone opens the front gate for me without a word through the intercom. I make my way back up, but I don't take the stairs; instead, I use the side ramp with a rubber surface, which seems like the easiest way to go up. I think of how it's not made for residents but for shopping carts; I ascend as if I were one. When I get to Daniela's apartment, she walks toward me, and for a moment I imagine my body to be weightless like hers. I don't know what I'm doing here, I say to her, but she doesn't respond. She just puts her arms around me and she rocks like a small vessel abandoned on a lake that's nearly still. My body is clad in a steely armor, like the thick rind of a giant fruit. She buries a knife directly into the crown of my head to cut it open; there's no need for her to slice downward to remove the peel. She simply twists, and that armor breaks open all on its own, forming one imperfect gash, zigzagging, capricious, splitting me in two with a crack. And it falls off completely, leaving everything bare: my eyes, my arms, my wideset hips that went unused during delivery, and the lingering weakness in my left knee from prenatal yoga. In the center of the sole of my foot I feel an effervescence, the kind I've seen discussed in traditional Chinese medicine, when a channel opens up for energy to flow through the meridians. Exposed, my body wavers, air-like, and in that ethereal movement Daniela kisses me. I don't know how to do anything, I tell her awkwardly, and we won't. I just want to be there as a farewell, to hold her as a reflection of a body and a life that will now no longer be mine. I feel the milk rising from my back to my shoulders, branching out until it engulfs me. I apologize for the kiss, foolish and past my prime, like an awkward old man. I'm a ghost witnessing a scene from a present that no longer belongs to me. I say goodbye just as awkwardly, but she seems so free, unsurprised as her body continues to sway. I wonder how Felipe and Antonia are, if they're wondering where I am, who I'm with, or if instead they're enjoying their break from me.

21

Felipe's mother insists on taking care of Antonia for more days of the week, which is such a relief because lately I can't catch a break from her crying. You're worn out from simply existing, she says. I use the time to go to the march; Blanca has put together a group with Daniela and her friends. We'll meet where the metro lets out, she tells me, as if that were feasible.

I sort through all the marches in my memory, arranging them in order. In the nineties there's Esther running with me in her arms, my little legs bouncing and banging against her hips. She throws her leather jacket over my head so I can breathe despite the cloud of tear gas the police fired into the crowd. We take shelter in the lobby of a building where she kicked past the concierge while cursing those milicos de mierda for the pigs they are. In the aughts, she and her friends protest in front of La Moneda shouting furiously that he died unpunished as I dance by her side to the beat of a bass drum. *Laura, you don't understand, there's nothing to celebrate.* Then came others, me in my school uniform, but by then Esther would just watch them on TV, cynical.

I walk down to the metro station—it's full of young women with bandanas and painted faces, singing and laughing in little groups, their tribes. Me, I'm still an island. Arriving at the plaza, I see women with their breasts covered in red blood, their faces behind sequined masks. My phone has no signal. I look around for Blanca and Daniela, but I can only see the tops of heads, hair blazing under the sun. I'm wearing leggings and a black shirt, and I regret it; I'm a stagehand, sweating and invisible, running around behind the scenes. Traditional Andean wear, girls with their green bandanas, street dogs, chants of No Means No. I try to make my way toward the center of the plaza, swimming through the bodies. Anonymized faces masked in black cloth, faded banners, buckets of water being thrown from the roofs and teens that welcome the drenching, their hands in the air.

I spot Daniela from afar standing with other girls dressed like her. She's naked from the waist up, her breasts freed. Her nipples are small and pale, like a young girl's; her skin, taut and smooth, appears not to sweat. She has her pink hair in a long Viking braid and, from what I can see, she has her eyes and lips made up and face gems between her brows. Blanca's dressed like me, a stagehand. Loudspeakers, bus stop trashcans getting kicked, girls dressed as nuns hugging a monument. Daniela calls out my name. Hairy armpits, handprints across mouths, drowned-out speeches on the megaphone, barricades, and the sun.

Blanca pulls me into a hug, and I laugh nervously like a little girl. No one marches forward, we're all just standing there swaying in a nervous mass. Daniela hands me a face covering, and I consider using it, I'm going to use it, but my body isn't working. I just clutch it to my chest, hiding it with embarrassment. I take off my shirt—one of the dozens the midwife made me buy for nursing, all of them awful—unbuttoning it furtively so no one sees my body, my asymmetry: my rejected left breast that Antonia refuses to take, shriveled, and my rock-hard right breast, bursting, both hang over my abdomen that's marred with a trench. I think: this body is not the one I had before, explaining myself when no one asked.

Naked women wave a purple flag over the great Baquedano and sweaty arms push into mine. We're burning tires, our smoke rising into the hot air and like a mirage our image warps in the heat; it's a desert. When the girls aren't looking, I slip the face covering over my head. It's tight on me, squishing my nose, and my hair sticks to the sweaty nape of my neck. I have a hard time breathing, but it's a refuge. I know Blanca's trying to catch my eye; she's smiling, which annoys me. I know she knows I feel ridiculous, but she lets me avoid her gaze, because that's her friendship: knowing me too well. And I know her. I know that she, like me, wants to forget the complexes for a moment, the being tied down by the body, wants to believe that we can also move unbridled and free like Daniela and her friends and all the girls around us. They shout, throw their hands in the air, jump, and sing as we flow down the Alameda, Santiago's main thoroughfare, like creeping lava. They shout again. My body feels rusted out, and I don't want to force it to dance. I just want to be there, walking alongside these women, to rest in the neutrality they offer me, to let them inhabit this body for me.

Tear gas is fired. The girls run, and I fall to the ground. Someone trips and falls on top of me. They grab my arm to get me up and I take off. Milk streams from my breasts and my heart beats wildly. Daniela yells out to me and I make my getaway. I throw on my clothes, anxious to get back and hug Antonia; there's this phantom feeling of her that clings to this body, a body which still does not belong to me. I feel guilty for having forgotten her. Ducking down, glued to the edge of the sidewalk, I make my way upstream through the bodies, desperate to get out, but euphoric, knowing I was there, although not fully present. But it looked like I was present, which for me, for now, is enough.

22

I unfollowed all the Instagram moms and left the lactation group chat without a word. I don't want any more theories. Felipe picks me and Antonia up for her monthly doctor's appointment. I don't care which doctor we see, I tell him, I just want to know she's okay. We drive along listening to the news, keeping the conversation light to avoid arguments, and I'm grateful. We catch up on what Antonia's been doing and what needs to be done at the house. The doctor measures and weighs her, I don't ask about anything else, and we leave with a sense of relief. Besides a bit of dermatitis, everything is fine.

Felipe thinks I look famished, so he asks to take me to lunch. It's the first time the three of us go out for food together. I'd been afraid, as with everything, that Antonia would cry if I took her to a restaurant, that she wouldn't let me eat, that people would give us the side-eye because of the noise or for showing my breasts, those kinds of awkward things. But the restaurant is empty. Felipe rocks her in his arms and she falls asleep. I gobble down my food in minutes—dumplings, chicken, Coca-Cola, watching her out of the corner of my eye to make sure she's okay—because I've gotten used to doing everything quickly: showering, getting dressed, running up the stairs, fearing the sound of her cry.

"I don't want to be away from you two any longer," Felipe says to me, setting her in the stroller. I try to come down from my hypervigilant state.

Time had never stopped for us like this before.

He takes my hand from its iron grip on my plate, and I swallow the soy sauce as I cry.

"And what you wrote in your text, it's not true."

"What text?"

"You absolutely can do this, and yes you *do* want to be a mom."

23

I spend the afternoon at home, alone, in a silence that's no longer so disquieting. Felipe's mother has taken Antonia out to a monthly luncheon with her friends, to show her off, and I use the time to organize things a bit before Felipe moves back in. Unrushed. His being gone these past few weeks has somewhat reduced my anxiety around keeping things tidy. You finally allowed a little room for chaos, he'll say. A waterfall of clothes is pouring out of the closet and damp towels hang over tops of doors. I no longer care.

In one of my drawers, I stumble upon Esther's box—it's following me. I finish looking through the handful of pictures from her past, the postcards from exile she never sent. The ones she did send were written and signed by Michel, with a cover name, and they never said anything specific, fearing someone could pin down who they were. But these ones, signed timidly with her initial, she wrote for herself. Even if she'd wanted to send them, she no longer had anyone to send them to; their sudden departure severed the ties they had in Chile, and my grandmother Nora, by the time Esther and Michel had settled in France, had already died from a heart issue she'd been dealing with for years. Camilo sent word of her death after they'd already buried her, in Santiago, far from her home. The very same day she received the news, Esther went to Père Lachaise and laid flowers on an unremarkable grave, imagining it was her mother's, to say goodbye.

March 1977, Pont Neuf

I'm carrying around a strange sadness, as if I'm here on borrowed time, visiting. It's hard having to adapt to so many things at once. The colors here are different, the air has a distinct smell to it, of nothingness and smoke ... Our suitcases remain unopened beneath our bed; we're always longing to return. Michel says that the victories of the enemy are not eternal.

E

May 1977, Gare Montparnasse

It feels impossible to learn the language well; you get used to managing with the little you pick up along the way. Michel claims you only need cuarenta palabras, just forty words, to begin making your way around. The Chileans nicknamed him El Cuarenta Palabras.

On weekends we meet up with friends at Toro's house, on Île de France. We call it Macondo; everything feels familiar there, and the gossip reminds us of Chile.

We miss the food; pantrucas soup noodles and our meatballs, they're nowhere to be found. We came across a little place where they sell a Serbian bean soup, reminiscent of our porotos, and we've taken to eating that out of pure nostalgia.

The French say: Rien où poser sa tête.

E

December 1977, La Nonette, Chantilly

"Paris was no party," Michel keeps saying, and he's right. It was just a bunch of soulless streets. The other Chileans did what they could to make us feel at home, but we preferred this move to Chantilly; it's a peaceful place. But what of La Habana? The heat I'd gripe about—incredible that now I miss it. I feel like I'm in a white jail; it seems we've been in winter for centuries.

E

The rest are postcards from her travels with detailed descriptions of every place they visited. *There's something of our north here in Granada, Norita, their people remind me of ours too, although Michel says I even see something of our Río Mapocho in the Seine.* There are also some pictures with friends from their exile, friends I don't know. One of them is taken in Place du Santiago du Chili—a picture of Esther and Michel holding up a banner that says: *from neither here nor there.* The last one is a picture from her childhood in Chile; my mother a tall, big-boned teen and my grandmother Nora small and stooped. Behind them is the Río del Choapa, a little north of Santiago. Written on the back: *childhood is when you put down your roots.*

24

"And there's no family left up north?"

My father looks over at the waitress bringing our plates while I'm trying to talk to him. He's old now, thinner. His shirt still pulls a bit tight across his stomach, but his face is no longer what it was; his skin is saggy, his eyes droopy. His blue has turned to gray, but he has that same lost look as always. Antonia's asleep in her stroller, and I'm using the break to get my father to focus and give me an answer.

"How could there be no one left?" I say, pressing him. "Camilo, you haven't kept up with him?"

"No. Could be he's dead, the son of a gun."

"Jeez, papá."

"Well, no one else," he says, irritated, picking at a piece of bread.

"And the house?"

"Should be there, I can't imagine it's moved."

He waits for me to laugh, but I don't.

"I'd like to go see it, bring Antonia."

"... Laurita, who knows where La Nena left that key ..." he says, referring to Esther. "I certainly don't have it." He puts his hands up like a thief caught red-handed.

Every time my father visits Chile we eat at the same restaurant. It's a small French place where they serve a lunch menu you could find anywhere, with the exception of the French onion soup. That's what Michel is slurping down now, hunched over the bowl, with the bread in his hand. I pull out the box of postcards from the hideous Peppa Pig bag. Michel puts down his spoon and wipes the oil from his mouth on his forearm. He's shaking, not from nerves, but from old age. His large, dry hands look rough as stone on the delicate cardboard box.

"*C'est quoi ça?* I don't follow."

"They're postcards, mamá's. Look at her handwriting."

He gives them the same look he gives the restaurant menu every time we come, pretending to read it when he already knows what he's going to order.

"*Je ne m'en souviens pas*, Laurita. What do you want me to tell you?"

The day we buried my mother we also came to this restaurant. Michel wanted to give me my belated eighteenth birthday present, for a birthday I'd unenthusiastically spent in the hospital a few months prior. His gift was a little Dutch doll that he'd bought in a *brocante* in Paris. The doll was glued down to a little piece of wood and lived trapped in a glass dome. I found it odd, and cute in its own way, but didn't thank him for it. We'd been talking more often since he'd found out about the cancer. He'd make brief, weekly calls to ask how things were going. I'd update him on the details of her illness, but at the first sign of a lull on my part, he'd say he had to go, anxious. He only spoke with Esther a few times. Nena, *j'en crois pas mes oreilles* ... was the only thing I heard him say on the other end. My mother shut the door. I like to think they had the heart-to-heart they owed each other.

When the doctor said it's time to say your goodbyes, Michel caught a flight, in an act of sound judgement that shocked me. Sometimes, in fits and starts, he's like that, and it's surprising. My mother was already unconscious. We made it in time to say our goodbyes to her in silence, the two of us kneeling beside one another next to her bed, watching as she faded away. Her skin was purple, her lips were dry, and her stomach was swollen with bile. We each gave her a kiss, but when it was my turn, I panicked. That body was already hard and cold, like church marble untouched by the sun. I remember thinking it wasn't true, the whole thing about the body staying warm and continuing to function after death. She went suddenly. Life wasn't subtle about it; it left her in a hurry. By then her body hadn't been fully there for months, her share of life little more than the meager light of a burning match.

I handled all the arrangements because Michel would just get into arguments with everyone over the phone. The young man at the funeral home asked if we wanted to wash or dress her, but both of us were clumsy, so he did it for us. Blanca's mother helped me with the rest of it. There was nothing symbolic about what we chose for her clothing and jewelry; we just wanted her to look beautiful. At the funeral, a woman sang Ave Maria—it was part of the song package—and those gathered, the gallá, as my mother would call it, were moved, despite being non-believers. As the song came to a close, Blanca's mother pulled me into a hug, plunging me into the fragrance of her coat, her warmth in sharp contrast with the chill of the chapel. Meanwhile, Blanca rubbed my shoulder as if to snap me back to reality. Then the coffin was lowered, and everyone cried in their own way, except Michel, who was still angry, despite being sad. Her work colleagues gave a speech, fellow members of her political party sang "The Internationale," and afterwards we all applauded. People waited until the very end—I suspect—for me and Michel to say a few words, but we didn't. We sent her off in silence, arm in arm like two frightened orphans. Blanca and her parents remained behind us, rendering themselves nearly invisible out of respect for us. As the coffin was being lowered, in a shadow far off from the chapel, I caught sight of Camilo. He'd put on weight, shaved his head, and looked anxious as ever. He tried to catch my eye, but I looked away in time. I pled silently for him to disappear, and he did; by the time my mother was in the ground, he'd vanished like a ghost.

In the days following her death, all Michel and I did was rest. I wanted nothing to do with the world because there was nothing to look forward to, so I locked myself in Esther's room and climbed under her duvet to sleep. I wrapped that duvet around myself three times, pulling it all the way over my head, to make myself sweat. There was something I found satisfying about sweating myself dry. The TV on nonstop, the blinds half open. Then Michel returned to France, and I decided that chapter was over. I washed the sheets, vacuumed, mopped the floor, cleaned the bathrooms with bleach, the windows with El Mercurio—the right-wing newspaper she complained so much about—and I shut her closet door, deciding that that life was over. Blanca thought I was being resilient, even though people didn't use that word then. I admire you, she'd say. But it wasn't fortitude, it was just a body hiding from the world, until further notice.

Antonia wakes calmly from her nap, pulling her little arms and legs in like a frog.

"Let me get a look at you, kiddo."

My father picks her up nervously. She grabs his face, and he lets out a theatrical laugh. Standing up awkwardly from the table, he lifts her into the air like Simba to show her to the restaurant owner, who looks over from the bar, smiling. They yell back and forth across the restaurant in an incomprehensible French, as Antonia laughs, looking beautiful. And it makes him look like a different man, a grandfather like any other. For the first time I recognize something familiar in Antonia's features; perhaps she also has a bit of my mother's lost spark.

"Have you ever been to the house?" I ask, interrupting him.

"Years ago! An ugly little dump," he says, clumsily handing me Antonia as he sits back down.

"Do you remember where it is?"

"Vaguely ... your mother always said I have a memory like a sieve."

He beckons to the waitress like he owns the place, asking for a pen, and then uses it to sketch on a cloth napkin—the owner lets everything slide. Touching the tip of the pen only ever so lightly to the fabric, he draws me a child-like map showing its location. The sketch is of a church, a long, dead-end side street, and at the end of that street, in a rectangle, he writes *casa*.

"There."

25

We're driving along the highway that borders the towering mountains—the ones that hold Valle del Choapa in an all-encompassing embrace. The drive stretches five hours over parched land with a dizzying climb. Felipe drives; I never learned how. Esther never learned either. She'd take taxis, even if she could hardly afford them, laden with books and her students' wrinkled up test papers that she'd spread out all over the seat. I'd sit up front because I hated dealing with all her stuff, and also because I wanted to keep clear of her cigarette smoke; she'd smoke with the window closed, so as not to mess up her hair. If she wasn't arguing with the taxi driver over politics, she'd be arguing over keeping the window closed. She had a knack for wielding a long ash, through turn after turn, the stop and go, meanwhile I'd be praying for everything to stay out of our way, afraid not of an accident, but of having that long ash fall on me. But it never did. Her provocations were nothing personal, she was just weary of a life that bored her. I suppose she tried to care for me in her own way, as well as she could, because despite the precarity of the ash, her lit cigarette never did burn either one of us.

My mind is on that memory when I ask Felipe if I can open a window, but please, what does he care? The wind comes buffeting in, sending everything flying: the yogurt box stuffed with our trash, the disposable cup with those last drops of Coke, and the napkins and bills we got back from paying the toll, dragging those last two out the window to be left fluttering over the highway. Felipe shouts, stressed, and Antonia wakes up crying, but I'm sorry, I need to breathe. We should've done this trip together, the two of us. It should be me and her in this car, opening the window, fighting, me asking her questions and her sharing who she was with me. We should've loved each other, yelled at each other, passed judgement on each other, looked each other in the eye, something. She should have been my mother, so I could have been her daughter. For years I felt the pain of that story that never was, the one I made up in secret, the one where I managed to save her from herself, from those cracks of hers, from her emptiness. A story where she managed to see me the way I always hoped she would. But life isn't made of those fictions; she and I were who we could be, in the time we had together. And this is my journey. Antonia and I are that bond. And look at us, we seem like a family. Felipe wants to hike up to a cave in the mountain where he says they practice witchcraft, and I want to lay on beds of quartz to align something, who knows what, whatever I need. If we don't end up doing any of that it doesn't matter, what does is that we'll always have this trip. Life will continue. Antonia will grow up, and there will be times when we're closer than others. And as she grows and I get old, our differences will become more and more apparent, and she'll find her own way, having her own life, perhaps her own family. And every now and then

I'll think back on the two of us riding along this highway and feel nostalgia for the bond we have now, because it will never be the same. Never again will we share this physical closeness, this intimacy. But that looming distance is not what's important right now; it doesn't make this moment any less meaningful, because being mother and daughter was never about that. It wasn't about upholding an absolute or struggling to stay in that absolute, nor was it about fulfilling a role or a mandate. It was simply about being present, even if distant or half-heartedly, but with honesty, which is the only way to really show up.

I feel dizzy. We pull over for a moment on the only shoulder where there's room to stop. I lie on the ground, in the shadows, while Antonia tugs at my hair and Felipe steps away to "use the bathroom." We're overlooking a reservoir, a treasure in this desert, but there's so little water that it doesn't show up in photos, so we leave with no evidence of that oasis. We stop at a rustic lunch spot along the way, and then arrive at the hotel by night, tired and a bit down due to the flour-heavy foods we ate: pan amasado, empanadas, and calzones rotos. This time I don't associate my feelings with anything dramatic, not with postpartum, my relationship with Felipe, or this belated grief. This is just my body reacting lethargically to the flour, nothing more.

We fall asleep watching a show we tried watching months ago; we could never make it through a single episode because of how exhausted we always were when we got to bed. I feel surrounded by neutral energy. The impersonal décor of the hotel room, it's saying nothing's wrong; all is well here. My body seems at peace, and I sleep dreamlessly, as if my consciousness has nothing left to cleanse. I feel no fear, rage, or anxiety, but rather surprise at this sense of calm—I almost find it suspect. At six in the morning, when Antonia awakes, we gaze calmly into each other's eyes. She wriggles like a fish trying to touch my face. Felipe has his arms around me. I don't want any of what we have here to fall apart. Perhaps what frightens me about this calm, what haunts me most, is the idea that for the first time everything in my life might be okay.

In the morning, we go down to eat breakfast in the hotel café. Felipe isn't up for doing anything in this heat, so I take the opportunity to go out with Antonia to get this done as soon as possible. I tell him we're off; he understands that Antonia and I need to be alone. Together we'll head into town and try to decipher the map my father sketched.

26

I arrive at the town's main plaza. There's a church and a small colonial building that's housing the town hall. Everything looks minuscule against the imposing backdrop of the cordillera that surrounds us. Antonia falls asleep in the baby wrap, rocked by my steps, and I'm relieved. I can relax seeing her sleep on my chest, most of all because I don't have to keep a constant eye on her, as if she's giving me a moment alone. I cover her head with a burp cloth, which doesn't do much, and as I walk along the dirt roads in the more than 95-degree heat I try to picture my mother walking alongside us. It's something I have trouble doing; my memories are fading, swirling together and contradicting one another. Perhaps there was a time when she was an unburdened woman, but in my eyes, she'd always been a mother drained of life, as if something were consuming her from within. And I don't mean the cancer, but a wound predating it, a hidden, silent crack that had always been there. And I inherited that emptiness. I've been carrying something broken ever since I was a mere extension of my mother's womb. A small fissure that compels us to silence, like a black hole that's there to remind us of how distance is always looming. Perhaps I grew in the part where she was broken. Perhaps my body took on the shape of that crack and a deep gashing hollow ran through my insides as if from an arrow or blade, which bends and twists as I move my legs. But Esther cannot have only been this; no woman is just a mother in silence. The door she closed between us concealed another woman, a way of being or a place to which she never allowed herself to return.

I keep walking, making my way uphill along a side street where a tall maqui tree leans out over the road. Up ahead, as if following the same route, there's an older woman, hunched over, moving slowly. She's wearing an apron over her clothes, her gait a little rough. I wonder if my grandmother Nora would've been like her. I rush to catch up and as she opens the door to her home, a small and simple wooden house, I ask after my family. She glances at my covered bundle—Antonia—bulging out from my abdomen like a turtle shell on backwards, and gives me a wary look. She waves me on indicating that it's still a few blocks further, perhaps just to get me to leave her alone, who knows. Regardless, it lines up with where my father marked on his map.

The house is small and old, near collapse. I walk into the yard through a gate wired half-heartedly shut. The garden is small too, but its flowers are cared for, although not by anyone in particular; they're native to this place, and they care for themselves. I take my time circling the house, peeking inside through the small open spaces between the boards nailed to the windows. It's crammed full of junk, equipment, and boxes, like a storehouse. Because that's what it is. Pinned up on one of the adobe walls, next to the front door, I spot a laminated piece of cardstock: it's a

Santa Teresa holy card. I start shaking. Antonia writhes about, uncomfortable, and wakes up. I sit for a moment beneath the maqui tree in the front yard and take her sweating little body out of the wrap to feed her. As she nurses, she scratches at my chest with tiny nails I forgot to cut. I cry a little, looking into her eyes, and hug her closely, as if asking her to hold me. I try to imagine what it was like to make a life here. My mother, my grandmother Nora, and other relatives I've never met. Esther must've been hoping to embrace those family members and friends after her return from exile, but that life and the country she'd left behind faded in her absence. A past life that I'll never know about, because this entire world died with her and now there's no one left to tell me the stories.

The journey doesn't end here.

Over the next few days Felipe will help me open that door so I can look through everything, but I won't find much I want to keep for now, just the Santa Teresa holy card, which will stay with me, replacing the medal I lost. We'll leave the house like that, boarded up, until we find time to make decisions, a time which is certainly not now. Felipe, Antonia, and I will continue exploring the valley; we'll hike up the mountain to the crack in the rock face where they practice witchcraft, and I'll take a nap on a bed of white rock, where a curandera will use her knowledge of traditional healing to tell me what I need, that I'm okay. We'll drive back to Santiago, to our home, to our life. But this journey will never end, because a part of me will remain sitting there, embracing Antonia beneath the shadows of that maqui tree overlooking the ruins of an unknown house, trying to understand who you were, what we were. The questions I have about you, your walled-off silence, the relationship you had with me ... There is no journey or memory, detail or fact, there are no postcards, pictures, or houses that can tell me who you truly were. There's so little I know about you for certain, and it will never be enough for me to tell our story.

Acknowledgements

To my mother Drina, my father Arturo, and the mothers and fathers of my friends from whom I took details of their stories to create this one. Also, to the phrases and images I borrowed from books, papers, and letters from exile that I came across along the way. To Alex June, a friend with whom I share my origin. To Carla Guelfenbein and those involved in her workshop for having been ruthless with the initial drafts. To the perceptiveness, generosity, and insight of this novel's first readers: Carolina Brown, Mike Wilson, Ana María Del Río, Sergio Infante, Mariana Schkolnik, Rebeca Chamudes, and Peti. To my editors, José and Nachito, for believing in this novel. To my literary friends Victoria Valenzuela, Lenka Carvallo, Montserrat Martorell, Vale Vlanco, June García, Caro Brown, and Mary Rogers: thank you for the support in those moments of despair. To Peti, my love and companion, and to his mother, Mariana (who is nothing like the character written here), for always being there for me. To the landscapes that are woven throughout this story: Illapel in Valle del Choapa; Macul in Santiago; La Habana, Matanzas, and the Isla de la Juventud in Cuba; Paris and Chantilly in France; and my grandfather's house in Supetar, Croatia. To the landscapes within of grief and postpartum. To my son Alonso, for accepting the solitude a mother needs to write.

Translator's Note

I began translating Chilean writer Catalina Infante Beovic in early 2020. Catalina was emerging as an author, and I as a translator, when my translation of her story "Ferns" (World Literature Today, 2020) became her first text to appear in English. In the waning days of 2022, she wrote to me with the soon-to-be-published copy of her debut novel, *La grieta*, and it was then that the gestation of this translation began.

I first read *La grieta* as a daughter, not yet a mother. I pored over the book, seeing a familiar refrain from Catalina's oeuvre, "we women," but this time she also wrote "we mothers," and I gleaned this unwritten sense of "we daughters," which evoked themes both poignant and relevant for any daughter, birthing person, mother, and their loved ones. These themes of motherhood and daughterhood are laid bare in this story, one that is grounded in the Chilean landscape and yet resonates across borders. In my countless readings of the story, I have found myself thinking of my mother and her mother, but now also of my daughter. Because unlike the first time I read *La grieta*, I am writing this note having given birth twice: first to my daughter and then to this translation.

My own matrescence informed my reading and translation of *La grieta*. Such shared experience is of course no prerequisite, but this translation, like any other, does indeed carry some part of me. Word choices such as the "dizzying thrill" of a fragrance during pregnancy, the "primal" look of the face during labor, and the "brush" of a daughter's fingers were pulled from my own pregnancy, labor, and postpartum, all of which I experienced while translating this work. My first drafts were written as my daughter grew inside me, and when, as written in these pages, "motherhood hit me blindside," I went back to revise armed with what my new motherhood continues to teach me. And throughout this process, carrying this translation to term while becoming a mother, I have been reflecting on my *grietas*, that is, "cracks," the ones I share with my mother and the ones I may come to share with my daughter.

The translation of the word *grieta*, and therefore the title, was but one of many challenges presented by this text, and the naming of something newly brought into the world is not to be taken lightly. That is why I so appreciate that my publisher and my editor, Christine and Shimanto, who are wonderfully collaborative, invited me to participate in the naming of this work and supported my proposal for the title on this cover. "Titles are one of the translator's many bugaboos," writes literary translator George Henson in his translator's note for Sergio Pitol's *Taming the Divine Heron* (Deep Vellum, 2023). He goes on to say:

> Curiously, while the title may be the last thing the writer writes, it is the first thing the reader reads. A title is never incidental. Never trivial. It is suggestive. It insinuates. It creates anticipation. It piques the reader's interest. It sets a mood.

La grieta could simply have been translated as *The Crack*, but I remain convinced that the suggestion, insinuation, and mood of such a title does not fit with the story held in these pages. The word "crack," firstly, is much more polysemic than the word *grieta*, which could create unintended ambiguity—an outcome we translators make a point to avoid. Other translations for *grieta*, such as "fissure," "crevice," and "rift," feel either too heavy-handed or incompatible with the way *grieta* appears throughout the Spanish-language text, a use I preserve throughout the English-language translation. And there is also the issue of how both words feel and sound: "crack" is a bit onomatopoeic with its monosyllabic explosiveness, and *grieta* is polysyllabic, bearing internal cracks, if you will. After much reflection I came to the conclusion that "crack" was the right word choice for translating *grieta*, but to allay my concerns with the word as a standalone title I decided it needed some company. The title *The Cracks We Bear* is a nod to Catalina's oeuvre with its use of "we" and also taps into the polysemy of "to bear," including the senses of "to give birth," "to carry," and "to endure," creating anticipation for the myriad ways that these cracks appear throughout this book.

The Cracks We Bear represents a novel debut for both author and translator, and my delivery of this translation has been guided by countless doulas, from my mentors and colleagues to my family and friends, and supported by Catalina's partnership on this journey. This book is born of both of us, author and translator, and as Catalina once told me: "It's as if we were writing together."

Michelle Mirabella
Pittsburgh, January 2025

MICHELLE MIRABELLA is a Spanish-to-English literary translator. Her work appears in the anthologies *Best Literary Translations* (Deep Vellum, 2024) and *Daughters of Latin America* (HarperCollins, 2023), as well as in venues such as *World Literature Today*, *Latin American Literature Today*, and *Southwest Review*. A former ALTA Travel Fellow, Michelle holds an MA in Translation and Interpretation from the Middlebury Institute and is an alumna of the Banff International Literary Translation Centre and the Bread Loaf Translators' Conference. Find more of her work at www.michellemirabella.com.

Book Club Discussion Guides on our website.

World Editions promotes voices from around the globe by publishing books from many different countries and languages in English translation. Through our work, we aim to enhance dialogue between cultures, foster new connections, and open doors which may otherwise have remained closed.

Also available from World Editions:

Río Muerto
Ricardo Silva Romero
Translated by Victor Meadowcroft
"A wrenching tale of murder and survival in Colombia
by an important Latin American voice."
—*Publishers Weekly*

This World Does Not Belong to Us
Natalia García Freire
Translated by Victor Meadowcroft
"Disquieting and visceral. (…) García Freire unearths
a brilliant sense of the miraculous from the swarming
and putrid subject matter. The result is beautifully
macabre."
—*Publishers Weekly,* *Starred Review*

Abyss
Pilar Quintana
Translated by Lisa Dillman
2023 NATIONAL BOOK AWARD FINALIST
"A triumph of perception and representation."
—National Book Award Judges Citation

The Bitch
Pilar Quintana
Translated by Lisa Dillman
2020 NATIONAL BOOK AWARD FINALIST
"*The Bitch* distills entire social, ethical, and cultural
universes into a potent short novel and offers a
startling, profound portrait of frustrated desire that will
stay with the reader for a long time to come."
—National Book Award Judges Citation

On the Design

As book design is an integral part of the reading experience, we would like to acknowledge the work of those who shaped the form in which the story is housed.

Tessa van der Waals (Netherlands) is responsible for the cover design, cover typography, and art direction of all World Editions books. She works in the internationally renowned tradition of Dutch Design. Her bright and powerful visual aesthetic maintains a harmony between image and typography, and captures the unique atmosphere of each book. She works closely with internationally celebrated photographers, artists, and letter designers. Her work has frequently been awarded prizes for Best Dutch Book Design.

The cover image was created by Francisca Álvarez Sánchez, a Chilean visual artist, illustrator, and educator. She has taken part in artist residencies in Mexico, Chile, and Spain, and in solo as well as group exhibitions. Her work spans artistic-pedagogical projects, theater design, stop-motion animation, editorial illustration, and mural art. Francisca Álvarez Sánchez writes about the cover image:

No me resistí
Me rompí
Me tuve que romper.

I couldn't resist
I broke
I had to break.

In order to give the cover image more impact and isolate it from its surroundings, designer Tessa van der Waals positioned it within a white border. She chose the typeface

Lektorat Display for the title and Lektorat Text for the author's name. The Lektorat font family, released in 2020 by TypeTogether, was designed by Florian Fecher, who won the 2019 Gerard Unger Scholarship with it.

Euan Monaghan (United Kingdom) is responsible for the typography and careful interior book design.

The text on the inside covers and the press quotes are set in Circular, designed by Laurenz Brunner (Switzerland) and published by Swiss type foundry Lineto.

All World Editions books are set in the typeface Dolly, specifically designed for book typography. Dolly creates a warm page image perfect for an enjoyable reading experience. This typeface is designed by Underware, a European collective formed by Bas Jacobs (Netherlands), Akiem Helmling (Germany), and Sami Kortemäki (Finland). Underware are also the creators of the World Editions logo, which meets the design requirement that "a strong shape can always be drawn with a toe in the sand."